TY

Vivian • Dot • Vale • Charles • Freeda • Harland • Doris • Jack • Matt Donovan • Carol

THE 27ᵀᴴ LETTER

a collection of stories of moderate length

Written,
Edited,
Compiled,
Created,
Designed,
and Loved
by

NICKI IVEY

ISBN-10: 0692220232
ISBN-13: 978-0692220238 (Ivey Books)

First Edition: May 2014
Published by Ivey Books
Northampton PA

Contents

Secret Ingredients

The ampersand was, not so long ago, recited by school children as the 27th letter of the alphabet. It grew from the letters *et*, which is Latin for "and". When *et* was written in cursive, the two letters were joined, and began to look quite a bit like the ampersands you will see scattered throughout this collection.

Letters, such as "a", "i", and historically "o", that were also words would be spoken and written proceeded with "per se", which means "by itself". So when children would recite the alphabet, you would hear "X, Y, Z, and per se and". In time, "and per se and" became slurred into the word we know now, ampersand.

A is for...anonymity

She woke up from her nap and stretched, her back arching and her head pressing into the soft back of the chair. Naps were wonderful. Only twenty minutes and one could feel refreshed as if they'd slept for hours.

Not that she was opposed to sleeping for hours. Hours spent in sleep were good, too.

She stretched her legs as well, and the rustling of fabric that was a singular sound, relegated to one particular garment, could be heard as loud as a set of cymbals crashing against her skull.

Her eyes snapped open.

Her hands flew to her lap.

She looked down, and saw piles upon piles of white silk and lace, her naked toes barely visible from

¶   Dear Joseph,

beneath the long gown. Her eyes were hypnotized by the intricate designs, the crystals that were woven into it.

Shaking her head, her gaze crept from the skirt to her torso, also clad in silk and lace, but instead of voluminous it was tight, constricting, and it stopped only an inch above being indecent.

Maybe half an inch.

Both of her arms were covered from her fingertips to just past her elbows in silk and lace as well, and there was heavy jewelry of some sort around her neck. She reached to feel the rows of heavy stones that fell into an arrow that pointed between her breasts. She could just see the dropped stone that was the feature of the necklace, and it matched a ring bearing the load of a very, very large, precious stone that was on her left hand.

She was confused. Why was she wearing a wedding gown? She did not remember getting engaged. That was something she was sure she would remember. It was something all young girls dreamed of—the moment their one true love got down on one knee, held out a little aqua blue or black velvet box and said those magic words...

"Ah, I see you're awake!"

She lurched up and out of the chair she'd been napping in, and spun to face the person behind the voice.

"Oh, now, did I startle you? Dear, I really thought we were past that."

¶ It has been nearly a month since my last

She stared at the man in the doorway. He was short—his head would barely reach her chin. He was ugly—his bulbous, red nose showed the result of years of indulging too much in his cups. Plus, she had no idea who he was.

It was right now that she realized there was more than one rustling sound going on. While the layers of her (admittedly amazing) dress slipped and shivered against each other, whispering to her to be careful, to watch out, warning her about the man she faced, there was also the clank and jangle of chains as she shifted her feet, backing away from the stranger.

She gathered some of the skirts, revealing her right ankle.

There was a white cuff, and a white chain. She had barely noticed it before, but now it weighed her down like an anchor.

"It's just for your protection, darling," the man in the doorway said, now moving through the room to a counter that held several decanters, each with a label she could not read. "You were so hurt the last time we let you loose. We just want you to be safe."

Hurt? She tried to test her joints, her bones, moving around to see what had been injured, but she found nothing.

"I don't feel hurt."

Her hands flew to her mouth. She wasn't sure what startled her more—that she had spoken, or that she didn't recognize her own voice. Her eyes darted around the room, and upon finding a mirror, she moved as

correspondence, but the time has flown by as if the

close to it as the chain around her ankle would allow.

Standing in the center of the room, looking at a large, floor-to-ceiling mirror, she nearly found herself in a heap on the floor.

She saw the gown, and recognized it as the one she currently wore. She saw the gloves on her arms, and knew they were her arms.

But she did not recognize her face. Her hair, a wild, spiky riot of short brown tufts was foreign. The nose that looked as if it might have been broken at one point was the one her fingers were feeling right now, but she did not know it to be hers. Even the color of her eyes were strange.

"What's happening? I don't understand. Why don't I know who I am?"

The man in the room held out a tall glass filled with an amber liquid. "Here, drink this."

She took it, but did not drink. "What is it?"

He shrugged. "I am not here to drug you, if that's what you think. It is merely something to help you feel better. You have been through a lot, and here you are now, on the day of your marriage to the most powerful man in the world. It is of course completely normal for you to be uncomfortable and confused."

Her head spun. She wanted to go back to the chair and go back to sleep, and hopefully when she woke again everything would make sense. She didn't dare move, because the thought of hearing the sound of the chain and of the dress again surrounded her with a blanket of paralyzing fear.

clocks have wings. My days are routine; I wake, eat

"Sweeting, drink. I assure you, you will feel better."

She looked at the glass, smelled the liquid, but could not bring herself to tip the glass.

He helped, with his slow movements and short stature, he was less threatening than her own towering reflection that was still facing her. His hand raised the bottom of the glass so the liquid flowed into her mouth. She didn't resist, and swallowed until the last drop slid down the back of her throat.

"Better?"

Agnes looked down at her manservant, and smiled. "Thank you, Abraham. That was just what I needed." Shaking her right ankle, she held it out from beneath her dress. "Could you please remove this now? I have a wedding to finish getting ready for."

Abraham smiled, and returned the glass to its place next to the decanter bearing the name of his mistress. He thought his master would be pleased with his choice for today. Such an important day deserved a polite, docile, willing woman. Putting the stopper back, he gazed at the other Personality Bottles, and thought perhaps later, he would use Aimee.

a small breakfast, then spend my days thinking of

you. My love, my heart swells when I remember your

ℬ is for...bashful

ettie never heard a crowd so loud in her life. The owner of the establishment was giving her directions, but she only saw his mouth moving. No words could be heard over the roar from behind the curtain.

Or maybe the noise was in her head. She couldn't be sure. Everyone else seemed to be conversing with each other just fine. The woman coming off the stage before her, wearing little more than a pair of low slung panties in an eye-blindingly bright shade of fuchsia, chatted with the stage manager before waving a cute hello in her direction that was accompanied with a wink. The dark-haired beauty who was to go on stage after her waved off whatever the lewd lighting director was sweating in her ear.

embrace, your touch. I regret only that I was not able

And all Bettie heard was a dull buzz that blocked out everything else. Like someone had strapped conch shells to her ears and added some speakers.

No, the noise definitely was in her head. It was a sound of regret, of guilt, of horror at the situation she had allowed herself to get in to. It had just seemed so easy...

And Bettie was simply that naive. To think that a criminal wouldn't miss illegally gained funds. Of course they would. They were the probably the only ones in the vast variety of clients Bettie had done accounting for who would miss it.

But they'd just had so much. It had been easy to move a little her way. Then a little more.

Then she'd got caught.

Yes. The white noise, the crashing cacophony...the guilt. That was what she heard.

Now they were gesturing to her. The stage manager first, a tall, wiry man who looked like he caught a bath about once every other week. His beard was thick, and probably was home to some very lucky vermin. Then the owner was waving frantically.

Bettie couldn't move until a very firm shove sent her stumbling on stage.

Maybe the sound of the crowd had been in her head, because Bettie couldn't see anything beyond the edge of the stage, much less people. But finally her hearing did start to clear up, because she could hear herself being announced.

Then the music started.

to give you a child while we were together for you to

Like a deer caught in headlights, Bettie couldn't move. She just stared, eyes wide, at the spotlights shining down on her, lighting her up like a Christmas tree. Her sequined corset shone. The sparkle of her spankies, similar in every way to what she'd worn with her cheerleader uniform five years ago in high school—except for the fact that they were designed to draw attention and not deflect it—felt like a target. The bra she'd been put in had more crystals than she'd ever considered putting on her body before.

All three were designed to draw attention.

To her.

Bettie.

Bookkeeper with a stupid streak.

Another woman was suddenly on stage with her, the one with the dark hair who was supposed to come on next. Did that mean she could leave?

Bettie tried moving towards the wings, but the brunette danced her back to the center of the stage. It was hard to not be hypnotized by the other woman's movements. She was swaying, rocking, enticing the crowd—whom Bettie could now hear, by the way—and telling a story.

She was entranced by it. She looked back at the crowd, the lights, then back at the brunette.

The crowd caught her small movement and cheered.

The brunette shook her finger at Bettie, shaking her head, then danced for the crowd for a moment before turning back to her.

remember me by. It was the ultimate gift I could not

She was on. Bettie was convinced. There was no crowd. They were there dancing for each other. A teacher telling her shy student what to do to please the customers.

With a toss of her hair, the brunette pulled apart the small vest she'd been wearing and peeled it off, rolling her shoulders and letting the garment slink to the floor. Then, spinning around to the crowd, gave them a wink and pulled Bettie upstage, away from the back curtains. They stood facing each other, profiled in the lights, as the brunette slid her way down to the board, unhooking the front of Bettie's corset as she went.

She couldn't help clutching the garment as the final clasp gave way, tugging it around her middle, standing precariously on four-inch heels. But the brunette slithered on the floor, jumping up behind her and snatching it away.

She tossed it out to the crowd.

They cheered at Bettie's performance, the perfect shy, virginal girl being instructed in the ways to arouse a crowd and bring in the money.

They had no idea how accurate this little show really was.

The brunette caught both of Bettie's hands, and started dancing a fake Tango with her, going against the music for a moment, meeting her eyes for a moment, then giving the audience a big, fake wink, which they loved. Bettie wasn't ready to be dipped, and she almost lost her footing when she felt herself being pitched backwards.

issue, and of course I blame myself. I curse my body for

The dark haired beauty was a pro, in more ways than one. Even in her own high heels, the other woman kept her balance, and when Bettie was pulled forward again, the bejeweled bra she was wearing slid down her arms, revealing pastie-clad breasts.

That was when Bettie could stand no more. Clutching her hands to her chest, ignoring the bra straps sliding toward her wrists, she stumbled off stage, her cheeks flushed red, a tear sliding down her cheek.

The crowd was actually doing the roaring this time. She could tell because the man who caught her, the man who decided that a little embarrassment would be good punishment for someone who was stupid enough to try to steal his money.

"You're pretty good at that, little Numbers," he said in her ear, tugging the bra off her arms and setting her back on her feet. "We'll have to work this into your regular schedule."

She choked. "Regular...what?"

He laughed at the expression on her face. "You thought I was just going to put you through this and let it go? Oh, no, Numbers. There's much more where this came from." He gave her a little push in the direction of the changing area for the dancers. "You go on and change and come up to my office. I have some business we need to go over."

Bettie stared at the man until he disappeared behind a door.

She almost wished she was back on stage.

Almost.

betraying you while my heart was in your hands.

¶   Alas, I cannot repair that mistake now in this letter.

C is for…coerce

arlita had always been fond of the comic character Nermal, Garfield's eternally cute and adorable nemesis. He was fond of flaunting the fact that everyone found him irresistible, and so was Carlita. He was not above using his looks to get what he wanted, and neither was Carlita. And like Nermal with his friend Garfield, many, many of her contemporaries wished she would disappear from the face of their world, shipped in a box to Abu Dhabi.

Or something like that.

Not that she could blame them. Carlita knew she was devious. She knew that other women's men were not safe around her, and that she could likely get them to do whatever she wanted. It was her special skill.

In fact, she was waiting for someone to come back

I will instead let my thoughts stray to your family.

with something she wanted just now. She was sitting outside in a small sidewalk cafe, wearing a little skirt that flattered her very long legs, her face balancing a pair of very large designer sunglasses on her pert nose. The awning kept her face in the shade, and the rest of her body gleamed in the sun, begging people on the sidewalk to turn their heads in her direction.

It was intoxicating, she would admit, and easy for less experienced women to get caught up in the novelty of all the attention.

But Carlita was a professional.

Ah, here came her young man now!

He was nearly as handsome as she was, with piercing eyes and a tall, athletic body that promised any woman that he would go the distance, if she wanted to spare the time. He walked the sidewalk as if he owned it, and people moved to the side so he could continue his long legged, confident stride towards his destination.

He came to Carlita's table, and didn't hesitate to lean over and brush his lips over her cheek.

She accepted the gesture as her due, as if he was kissing the ring of the pope instead of her face.

Well, it was her due. She deserved respect.

Those who didn't respect Carlita usually ended up in quite a bit of trouble.

"I have what you asked for," her companion said as he positioned himself at her side.

She did not want it out on the table.

"Not here," she said, sliding the envelope and his hand that covered it off the surface. "Place it in my

¶ How does your mother fare? I remember what

purse, please."

He did as he was asked, not missing a beat, not making a scene. The small package was delivered to its home. Where it belonged. How could it have ever been in the possession of anyone else, when it was so obvious to him, and of course everyone else, that it belonged to her?

Carlita smiled. Behind his piercing gaze, she saw his thoughts. They were so transparent, so easy for one such as her to see.

"Thank you, you may go," she said, releasing him from her power. He lingered for only a moment, hoping for any sign, any token of her affection that she might pass his way, but there was nothing. Only her perfect, serene smile.

She watched the young man walk away, back to his life. Back to his little problems, and his little girlfriend, who of course would probably not be at all happy that her great-grandmother's pearl and diamond necklace was no longer in the safe where it had been just last week, when she had shown her fiancé the treasure.

But there was nothing anyone could do about it now. He would go home, and she would accuse him. He would not know anything, swear on his life, his own grandmother's life, that he had nothing to do with it.

And when they discovered his fingerprints on the safe, he would swear he had been set up, but would have no explanation as to who could have done it.

The engagement would be off.

Her heart, and her family's fortune, would be

seems like forever ago that she was mourning the loss

broken.

And Carlita's young man would be tortured to an early grave about the vaguest dream of an exotic woman who asked him for a favor.

Carlita smiled at the thought of his sacrifice for her. He was so sweet to have done such a thing. But now she needed something to wear with it. Perhaps a new gown? She watched the crowd walk by on the sidewalk, and saw him on the other side of the street.

Looking through her glasses, she allowed her gaze to fold deeper into him, to see the things no one else cared to notice. The things her charm allowed her to see.

He was an apprentice for the most desired fashion designer of the day. He was on his way to work, and about to cross the street. More importantly, he was younger than she by a few dozen years, he was handsome, and his will, while not weak, would never stand against hers.

Carlita and her ageless beauty gathered her scarf and bag, tipped her sunglasses to the top of her head and pulled down her hair. It was how he liked his models and muse to look.

Free, young, fresh.

Not even the breeze was fresher than Carlita just now. Despite the fact that she was nearing a century in age.

Young, for her type.

Two measured steps then one awkward one sent her tipping in to her next mark.

of her youngest brother. It is unfair to be torn from the

Perfectly choreographed.
"Oh!"
He caught her.
And then he looked at her.
And she caught him.

ones you love before you are ready to let go, but that's

how the world treats us all. I send her not sympathy

$\mathcal{D}$ is for...daughter

$\mathcal{D}$eedee was late.

Her car, a bright pink sports car with two seats and no functional trunk, sped up to the door of her father's building. The tires screamed and rubber burned as she slammed on the brakes just inches from the curb. Climbing out, not caring about poise or presentation, her dress slid up her thigh to dangerous heights.

She didn't pay attention to the valet as she scurried past him, her heels clacking on the cement.

Then she squealed.

"Wait, wait!" She hit the back of the car with the palm of her hand just as it was pulling away, and thankfully the valet stopped.

Deedee pulled open the passenger door and

but strength to make it through this hard time.

grabbed her purse. "Thanks!"

She didn't close the door behind her, running back towards the glass fronted building.

The door, thankfully, was opened for her by one of her father's many bodyguards who was presently masquerading as a doorman.

Like his disguise would fool anyone.

She ignored him, too. The bodyguards working valet and doorman, they were inconsequential. The ones who needed her attention were directly in front of her.

"Hey, boys!" She was chipper, her smile was big, and as she leaned over the granite counter, her toes lifting off the floor, she gave both men a good view. "I'm here to see Daddy, but I'm sooo late!"

"Miss Deidre, your father is waiting for you," the tall one responded with a flat tone.

They were paid to not notice that she was practically flashing them right now, even though she was trying to make it impossible.

Deedee gave a huge sigh. "I know," she pouted, leaning forward a bit more. "Can you please, please call up to his secretary and have her cover for me? And then you can take me up in his elevator. I know it's the fastest."

The short, thick one, known for his strength and ability to intimidate nearly everyone, looked at his partner, unsure. "Miss Deidre, we can't."

"Are you sure? I'm never going to make it in time on the regular elevators! Unless one of you comes with me

¶ And your sister? She and I had been so close at one

and uses his pass? Then you wouldn't get in trouble,
and neither would I!"

Her sweet smile and the extra flash of cleavage swayed the tall one, although he didn't waver from his hard exterior. She followed him to the elevator, and walked in after him.

Her heels were loud in the small space, but Deedee couldn't help but pace in tiny circles. She was nervous. Who in their right mind wouldn't be? He was the head of one of the most violent crime syndicates in the country, and definitely the most controlling and viscous in the city. And even though she was his daughter, she wasn't immune from his anger.

And when you were summoned to his office, even if you were his daughter, you had reason to be nervous.

She watched the floor numbers growing higher and higher. Her thoughts were spinning, and it showed on her face. Anxiety, frustration, impatience. And a vague confusion that was always part of Deedee's expression.

Thirty-one. It was her father's floor. Not the top floor, because that was too vulnerable.

Deedee preceded the bodyguard out of the elevator. He followed her just long enough to make sure she was in the presence of her father's secretary, then went back to his post.

No corner office for Franklin Korman, and for the same reason he didn't have a top-floor office. He didn't get as far as he had by being stupid. The building was state of the art in terms of defense. None of his enemies had been able to get to him, and they tried

time, but with the distance now between us, things are

more than once to get at either the man at the top or his information.

Deedee looked at her father's secretary, a woman only a few years older than she was. She was attractive, of course, but beneath the conservative dress, Deedee knew lurked the heart and body of a killer.

She wouldn't doubt that there was a gun trained on her right now as the woman paged her father to let him know his daughter had arrived.

A button on the secretary's desk triggered the release of her father's door from the reception side, and another code from inside the room released a separate lock, allowing the doors to swing open.

Deedee walked through, smiling, vague, and eager to see her father.

<!-- * * * -->

Molly sat in reception, keeping one eye on the security cameras for her floor and one ear on the discussion in the other room. It was her job to protect Mr. Korman, even if that meant protecting him from his small-brained daughter.

She couldn't help but be disgusted by the girl. She was stupid, and that was all there was to it. Molly could not stand weakness.

She listened to Deidre try to defend herself against her father's accusations, but there really wasn't anything the girl could say to make what she did right.

Deedee had done the worst thing any daughter

not the same. They never can be, I suppose. If things

could do to her father.

She had made him seem weak in the eyes of the public with her stories of her beloved, kind father. While he had worked his entire life to intimidate and punish and be feared, his daughter worked to destroy it with her lack of forethought.

And now Mr. Korman was doing the only thing he could do without ordering Molly to kill his daughter on her way out.

She turned her attention back to the video feed displayed on her left monitor when Deidre Korman left her father's office. The doors shut automatically, with a click of finality. Out of the corner of her eye she could see the tears on the girl's cheeks, and she couldn't help the twinge of disgust at the weakness she was showing.

But Molly didn't hear any sniffles.

And even though Molly was a trained killer, she was still a woman.

She looked at Deidre closely.

<!-- * * * -->

Deedee knew what Molly saw. She let her. She didn't have to pretend any more.

"Would you call for my car, please?" She pulled a mirror out of her purse and dabbed at her eyes, careful not to mar her makeup.

It was perfect, and now her life was, too.

No more mob.

always stayed the same, we would not grow as people,

No more death.
No more crying silently in the middle of the night.
She had been disowned.

Molly watched the happiest devastated woman she'd ever seen walk into the elevator, and knew that for her, it wouldn't be that easy to get out.

but be stuck in the same, miserable situations our

entire lives.

¶   That's not to say that I consider my previous

E is for...eviction

"Empress, we are ready."

There was a sound of rustling fabric. Long, full robes made of exotic fabrics brushed against each other and the floor, sweeping along the marble hallways.

"Good," the Empress replied in a dramatic contralto voice. It was a voice of power, and she reveled in it.

They walked along the tall corridors, built to accommodate the height of the reigning Empress and her family. While her entourage and all servants in her palace and the grounds were of average height, the Empress always towered above them.

Their destination was the interior of the palace, to where a glorious courtyard awaited them. It contained the rarest of flowers and vegetation, an elevated

situation miserable, of course. You must never think

platform for the Empress, and was always supplied with her favorite foods and drinks. The Empress should never be without basic needs, no matter how mundane or horrific the arena that demanded her attention.

She never raised her robes, but her steps were sure, finding each paving stone leading to her throne, never letting her feet touch anything alive. Her power came from the stone, from the earth. Not the plant life that lived like leeches on its surface.

The people who had already gathered in the courtyard watched her. Some knew that her robes hid the body of an athlete; strong, powerful, fast.

Deadly.

Others only saw what the Empress wanted them to see; someone used to pampering, fragile, delicate.

She didn't care what they saw. She knew that eventually they would all bow to her. If they didn't, they would end up like the souls she was about to evict today.

With a quiet sweep of her robes, the Empress sat in her throne. Large, made of marble and granite, impenetrable. Like her.

A court herald stood on her left, and began the proceedings in his loud, carrying voice.

"We are here today in the presence of her most exalted highness, the Empress, to send three vile, ignorant liars to their final rest. Is there any here today that would argue for their lives?"

The only sound was that of the birds that the Empress allowed to live within the walls of her palace.

that of me. You were my life, Joseph. I don't know how

One sang a sorrowful tune, as if it knew what fate awaited the criminals and felt sympathy for them.

The other made a strange choking sound, pretended to die, then flew up to the highest spot in the courtyard, alighting on the Empress' throne.

"Then you are sentenced to freedom," the Empress declared to the three who now stood before her. "Leave my palace, and never return."

None of the three gave any expression to either please or antagonize the Empress. They turned as she raised her hand, opening the gateway that led to their freedom.

The Empress' Labyrinth.

<!-- * * * -->

Ellie looked at Edgar and Eunice. "Seriously, guys, what are we going to do now?"

Edgar looked at the two women, then, snapping a branch from one of the trees that made up the thick, impenetrable walls of the maze, started pulling the smaller branches off. "I think it'd be a great idea if you two volunteered to be cat food so I could escape."

Ellie reached out and slapped Edgar.

He caught his reddened cheek and smiled. "Okay, well, it wasn't my best idea."

Eunice looked on the verge of panic. "There's no way we can make it out of this, is there?"

Edgar shrugged. "Just because we've never heard of anyone making it out before doesn't mean nobody has.

else to say it, or how to convince you of it. I breathed for

The Empress probably makes sure nobody hears about it if anyone makes it out."

"No, no, we would hear. We were the top, you know? The closest to her, the ones who heard everything first. And we never heard, right? We never heard!"

Eunice actually lost it at that point, sobbing on Ellie's shoulder, clutching a woman she hadn't been able to stand back in the palace. A woman she had actively loathed.

Ellie just stood there, patting her back, staring at Edgar helplessly.

Edgar shrugged. He'd never liked Eunice, and wasn't willing to start pretending now.

He had managed to hide a blade in his pocket, or maybe the guards had been interested to see a little bit of fight in the food they were sending out. Now he went to work on the end of the branch he'd pulled from the wall.

He didn't look back at the women, simply started walking. Ellie managed to get herself free of Eunice, and while she felt bad for the weeping woman, she was more concerned about her own survival.

She grabbed a branch from the wall and started imitating Edgar, stripping down the branch in her hands, following in his footsteps.

Eunice, upon realizing she was being left behind, managed to get a grip on her waterworks and followed as well.

you. I ate for you. And even now, though I am growing

It truly was a maze, and one designed by a master. Fortunately, Edgar was a bit of a maze master himself. He'd never designed something children needed to trace their way out of, or that he ever expected having to fight his way out of for that matter. But he'd worked with information mazes, and there was always a way out. A pattern.

A method to the madness.

He ignored the women trailing behind him, focusing on sharpening his spear, handing it back to Ellie who would provide him with another stripped branch and pass the finished spears to Eunice. It possibly wasn't the brightest idea giving the mentally disturbed woman the weapons, but he couldn't waste time worrying about it now.

Left turn. Left turn. Right by default. Left turn. Left turn. Even when it was obvious they were walking into a dead end he turned left, left, and left again. Patterns were important. Constantly making the same turns would get them out eventually.

Or to the heart of the maze. The center, where the Empress' pet awaited them.

No one knew exactly what the Empress kept in her labyrinth. They knew she liked birds in her courtyard, and dogs in her bedchamber. She preferred the art to always be feline, but no one had actually seen a cat in the palace. Which was why everyone assumed the pet in the maze was a cat.

A very large cat. A very scary cat. A very deadly cat.

weak as time passes, I live only for you.

But still, a cat.

Left turn, left turn, left, left, left. It felt much like a bad rhyming book Edgar had once read to his niece, Elise. But he kept on, kept moving.

And finally, armed with fourteen spears that Edgar was pretty sure neither of the women knew how to use, they found it.

¶ This life now is miserable. My thoughts stray

constantly to what I cannot have, to what I am denied

because of my own actions. I regret it with every breath

$\mathcal{F}$ is for...feline

$\mathcal{F}$elicity left the lab late. It was a habit for her—she'd never been much of a morning person, especially since her surgery. Even during her months of recovery she ended up watching the late late shows and infomercials instead of getting up early and getting a move on her therapy.

Which is probably why it had been six months instead of the promised three before she was finally released.

She didn't let it bother her, though. She was free now, and it felt good. She had been working for six months learning how to use her new body after her "accident".

She was pretty sure someone had run her down on purpose.

I am allowed to take, but I cannot...

But she didn't let that bother her, either. In fact, remarkably little bothered her any more. She was concerned about when she ate, and whether her food was fresh, and irritated when someone woke her up from one of her frequent naps. And she hated when one of the other patients at the rehab center came into her room

That was it. She was content ninety percent of the time.

Now she was out hunting. The lab had done a pretty good job of recreating the ground surfaces she would encounter outside, so her bare feet weren't bothered by the rough concrete or stones that littered the landscaping. The grass felt heavenly, and she thought about just flopping down and rolling in it, trying to pull the coolness from the blades and let it soak into her.

But she was hungry. She needed to hunt. So she resisted the grass.

Things looked a bit strange through her new eyes. She couldn't see nearly as far, and colors weren't nearly as vibrant, but it was more than made up for by her increased perception of movement.

And the fact that while only moonlight lit the landscape, she was seeing just as well if not better than she had in the hospital.

She was going to have to thank the doctors for that.

Or not. They knew what they were doing, and in a fashion, so did Felicity. She felt a little like Bridget Fonda tonight, being tested in *Point of No Return*. She

¶ I cannot change the past. I cannot change what I

was searching for food, but it was actually much more than that.

It was a test. A test to see how well their little experiment worked.

Felicity rolled her shoulders, feeling the harness that held the gun strapped to the center of her chest. The first attempts had been to use a harness similar to that used by human police, with the gun strapped under her arm, but her new body balked at that.

Walking on all fours, having a cold piece of metal and some stiff leather rubbing between your elbow and side was inefficient.

She flicked her tail at the memory of having to try that particular combination for a week before they let her remove it.

Not at all pleasant.

They had settled, upon her request (and a little veterinary common sense), with a similar harness that had a pocket for the pistol against her ribs. She was right-pawed, as she had been right-handed before, and she could easily grab the gun with her new, modified appendage.

She was a better shot than before as well.

Eyesight, strength, whatever.

She was better.

She saw some movement to her left ahead of her. She had traveled quite a distance from the lab, and now was moving into a suburban area.

Felicity had used to live here, hadn't she?

It was familiar and foreign at the same time. The

have done.

longer she spent in this new body, getting used to the way it worked and what it could do, the harder it became to remember anything before the accident. It had only been six months, but that part, the Before...it was just fuzzy.

Following the movement, she wandered silently between trees, jumping over a fence or two, inspecting strange smells, then moving on.

The person she was following was going somewhere familiar. While the human walked along the sidewalk, Felicity kept pace, catching glimpses of movement from between houses.

She stalked him all the way to a house.

His house.

But in the back yard, where she held court from the solid branch of a very old tree, she felt something familiar.

It wasn't his house, it was hers.

There was a key hidden under the back mat. Since the yard's fence was high, Felicity had thought—Before—that it had been a safe place to put it. It was easier to scale a fence than to hire a locksmith, she remembered thinking.

Now with her new body, it was easier than she'd ever expected.

Slinking up to the porch, she sat back on her haunches and picked up the mat.

The key was still there.

Opposable thumbs were something the team of surgeons and scientists thought she would need, and

¶   I don't know why I keep writing to you. It's obvious

indeed they were coming in very helpful right now. She unlocked and opened the back door as quietly as she had moved through the neighborhood. She waited for a moment, evaluating the kitchen she was now faced with, waiting for movement.

Hadn't she had a pet?

There was a small body hunched beneath the table on a chair. It was Fiona's favorite spot.

Felicity walked on all fours, leaving the back door open, approaching her former pet.

Fiona was alarmed at first, her hackles raising, and Felicity felt her own raise in defense.

But she wasn't all feline. She calmed herself, and waited. Fiona stuck her head out towards Felicity, smelling the air.

Trying to determine why this human-sized feline predator smelled so familiar.

The front door opened, and startled both of the cats. Felicity ran under the table, Fiona ran out the back door.

It would be better this way.

The man who had entered Felicity's home dumped his keys on the table by the door and threw his coat towards the coat tree, but missed.

Felicity tried not to hiss.

She recognized him now. He certainly hadn't changed in her absence.

Walking to the kitchen, he walked past the doorway to the darkened dining room, oblivious to Felicity's presence. When he saw the back door open, he swore.

that you're not going to respond. But now it's become

"Fiona! Here, kitty!" And when Fiona didn't immediately appear, "Screw it. Stupid cat better take care of itself," and he slammed the door.

But didn't lock it.

She heard him sigh and open the refrigerator, opening the can he pulled out.

He still drank that cheap crap, Felicity thought as she smelled the stink of his beer. It had always bothered her when they were together that he would drink a can right before coming upstairs to get intimate, never offering to brush, even when she asked.

"Honey, is that you?"

This time Felicity couldn't help her reaction when she hissed and her fur rose to double her size.

What was a woman doing in her house?

And then she remembered.

She remembered what she had come home to that day about six and a half months ago—her fiancé and another woman, in her bed.

She remembered getting in her car, and driving away to the sounds of her husband swearing and insulting her for being cold, frigid; a limp noodle in bed.

And Felicity remembered the last face she'd ever seen as her car was T-boned in the center of a very busy intersection only a few blocks from her house, about a week after she left.

Her first test? To kill the lying, cheating dog who had forced her into this new life.

A new breed of hunter indeed.

habit, and so I continue. Part of me blindly hopes that

you will return my letters, but when I use my head

instead of my heart, I know you won't.

G is for...guardian

*I*n some video games, the longer you stay alive, the faster things move. Response times must increase, the difficulty notches up, and adrenaline spikes through the player's body.

Glory was definitely feeling those spikes.

Her avatar was chasing another player through the game field. They were on the same side, but Glory was after him just the same. The moment he stumbled upon a treasure hunter, the antagonist in this game, her avatar killed them both with a well-placed gunshot.

She immediately left the scene of the crime. The longer she stayed, the sooner the other Ghost Guardians would find her and declare her rogue, going after her instead of the treasure hunters.

She needed to find it before they did.

¶ I want you to know that I miss you, and that there

The treasure.

The game's ultimate goal.

Ghost Guardians had started out a humble arcade game. One player attacked computer-generated treasure hunters and tried to scare them out of the haunted mansion. Game play continued until the computer found the treasure, or until all them had been scared off by the player-controlled Guardians.

As technology evolved, so did the game. Ghost Guardians started guarding different locations, and the treasure hunters evolved into playable characters. Finally, multiple Guardians could play in one massive online game, working together to win points and tokens that they could then trade to customize their avatars.

Glory, and a few like her who had been playing the game since it's creation, had a theory that many dismissed. It was denied especially by the game's creators. They theorized that the ultimate goal in the game wasn't to scare off the treasure hunters, but to find the treasure before them.

Glory felt she was very close to proving this theory.

She raced down a hallway and paused, just before rounding the corner, leading with her gun hand. She whipped around, took a glance, then snapped back when a shot rang out at her head.

A treasure hunter had found her, and was on the attack.

The hunters that were being played by gamers were usually not quite as clever as the computer generated

is no thing I would most like to change in my life than

versions, so Glory left a precious grenade behind where she'd stood, then retreated out of the blast range. She was rewarded by bloody bits of hunter raining down across her screen, and the yowl of rage in her ear from the player who had just died.

"Sorry," she mumbled into her headset as she raced forward now that the coast was clear. Another quick check of the hallway found it empty.

She had made it this far before and died. Now her fingers tingled in anticipation, her heart raced, and other players could hear her soft panting in their ears if they were close enough to listen.

There was a hidden door here, and although these were frequent enough, this one, when opened from the wrong side, sent her through into a maze.

It had been booby trapped before. This time she made a careful sweep of the doorway after she opened it, having her avatar remove and slide a shoe in across the floor before stepping in.

Nothing.

The door swung shut behind her, and Glory's avatar picked up the footwear as she swept past, the shoe appearing back on her foot the instant she touched it.

It was all about left turns, and looking for things that appeared too normal. Out of place was easy. Amateurs left things out in the open. The game designers would have more traps for her in the most innocent of areas.

Glory avoided the plant urn, circling it, never turning her back on it. When a flower twitched, she shot it with her machine gun to reveal the body of a

how I behaved at our last meeting. It was, and will

bloodied hunter slumping out of the shape it had been crammed into. Then, whipping around with a sword in her hand, Glory was able to catch the next hunter just under the chin, severing it's head from it's body. She had to drop the long blade when her swing caused it to lodge in the woodwork of the hallway she was walking through, trading it for two smaller blades that pierced through the armor of the third and fourth hunters waiting to attack.

Decorative shelves indicated head-high dangers, and Glory's avatar crouched through the area, watching darts fly above her head. At the end, she jumped on a hunch, and was rewarded when the floor fell away beneath her. She barely managed to land on the opposite ledge, where she was faced with a door.

The final door.

If it was possible to dream about a doorway in a video game, Glory had done it. And this door she was now faced with fulfilled every fantasy she might have had.

It was elaborate. It was mesmerizing.

And it was locked.

In the center of the door was a circle, and inside this circle was a cut out of the first weapon featured in the Ghost Guardian's in-game store ever. It was a simple dagger, and easily purchased. Since your player could only hold a certain number of weapons, nearly everyone resold this particular item after gaining better, more deadly items.

Glory pulled hers out from her arsenal. There was

always be, the worst choice I have ever made.

a feather carved into the hilt, the symbol the treasure hunters wore.

She lined up her dagger with the inset carving on the door.

She was rewarded with the clicks and clatter that came with heavy internal mechanics.

Glory couldn't have moved her gaze from her screen if she tried. When the door opened and she was faced with the pitch black beyond it, she didn't hesitate before moving her avatar through.

And then there was nothing.

Almost literally.

The lights in Glory's apartment were extinguished. The constant buzz of the air conditioning unit went silent. Her fan went off, and the custom back-lit controller in her hands lost all life.

But she could still hear ambient sounds in her headphones, and the monitor she had been staring at for the past ten hours now displayed a single point of light.

A flame growing in the distance as if looking down a long, black tunnel.

The words at the bottom of the screen were polite.

Please wait.

She only needed to sit quietly for a few moments before there was a knock on Glory's door.

<!-- * * * -->

"So, you've found it."

¶ I'm sorry I killed you.

Glory nodded. She was in a room with boundaries that she couldn't define. She sat at a table, a glass of water within reach, and a single light shone down on her.

She could see nothing beyond her circle of light, but she had no doubt that *they* could see *her*.

"What are you planning to do now?"

Glory's pulse pounded, and she shrugged, careful not to seem either disinterested or obsessive.

"You have heard the rumors, I assume?"

"I created the rumors," Glory answered honestly. She was the first to question the goal of the game. She was the first to connect the clues she found during both game play and offline. "I was the first."

A second voice made a sound of approval. "So you will accept our offer?"

Glory couldn't stop the smile that crossed her face. "Put me in the game."

<!-- * * * -->

Glory's body wasted away. The wires leading from the skeletal body to the computer bank had more substance, and were more attractively arrayed. Bundled in wrist-thick cords, tied together to prevent tangling, they took Glory out of her body, and into the computer.

Her avatar, her character, Glory herself, was unbeatable. Rumors flew among the human players about the gamer who had become part of the game.

¶ With my confession plainly spoken, I hope you can

Glory heard it all. Every conversation, every gossip, all the idle chatter, whether it was in the game or elsewhere online.

She made the game better. She made the game unbeatable.

Glory *was* the game. The Ghost Guardian Goddess.

find it in your heart to forgive me.

¶   Eternally yours,

$\mathcal{H}$ is for...horse

$\mathcal{H}$ilda and her stallion galloped through the house at top speed. The smooth marble floors presented no problems for the sure footed, unshod steed as it leapt over tables and managed sharp corners leading to wide corridors.

She threw her head back and screamed her thrill at treating her fathers house this way. Never mind that Hadley had nearly taken out a maid or two. As Hilda saw it, they were all adulteresses anyway, and deserved whatever they had coming to them.

Eventually, her way was blocked by the only other mistress Hadley would recognize.

Hilda's mother.

"Hildy, stop this," her mother commanded as Hadley was brought to an abrupt halt.

"He won't stop—why should I?"

Her mother took her daughter's horse by his bridle. "Because this is not your fight. It's mine."

Hilda pulled on Hadley's reigns, causing the powerful creature to rear up in objection. "Then fight it," she told her mother with all the pent up venom she'd been holding for her father. She turned Hadley, and galloped off in the direction she had come.

<!-- * * * -->

"You know she's just trying to protect you, right?"

Hilda stood in the middle of the forest next to the tallest horse most had ever seen, brushing his coat and cooling him down.

When he spoke, she rested her head on his neck.

"I don't care," she mumbled into his softness. "I don't need protecting. I have you."

Hadley shook his head, sending a butterfly to the skies. "You won't have me forever. I'm not immortal, you know."

Hilda shuddered at the reminder. He wasn't. Her best friend in the world would leave her far before she was ready.

While he wasn't immortal, she was.

And so was her father, damn it.

"She shouldn't try to protect me. He'll just hurt her. I need to protect her from all of his philandering."

Hadley put his head around her shoulder, comforting her as best he could with his warmth. "She

<!-- * * * -->

knew what she was getting into when she married him."

Hilda took a step back, then, stiffening, straightening, pulling herself together.

"Of course she did. She knew he was a lying cheat from day one." She wiped her sleeve across her eyes before resuming the rhythmic motion of brushing her horse. "And yet she still got involved with him."

"If she hadn't, you wouldn't be here," Hadley pointed out.

"If she hadn't," Hilda countered, "she would never have had to endure having the man she once loved rip her heart out over and over again, just because he can't keep his pants zipped."

Hadley didn't answer this time.

Hilda saw him go perfectly still, and became motionless herself.

There was no sound, and that's what had caught Hadley's attention.

She was a hunter, and he a hunter's steed. She knew how to fight, and how to defend herself.

She slid the brush into one of the many pockets adorning her long coat, and silently wound her hand in Hadley's long mane. If he took off, she would be with him in a heartbeat.

<!-- * * * -->

Hudson walked through the thick brush as if he was floating over it. In fact, he actually was a little bit. When

¶ Sitting at her small secretary by the fire, Mathilda

travelling in strange lands it wasn't always a bad idea to not announce your arrival. One never knew who or what would be waiting past the next brier bush.

So he floated, only about an inch or so off the ground, and he made no noise. But since the mode of transportation often took quite a bit of concentration to maintain, he didn't see danger until he literally ran right into it.

The tip of a sword pierced through his jacket and shirt, drawing a pearl of blood from his chest before he managed to stop his forward progress.

He found himself staring into a pair of devil's eyes. They were red, dancing with flames, and filled with fury at having been trespassed upon.

Hudson jumped—well, flew—back with force, slamming himself into a tree, knocking the wind out of his chest.

Gasping, dragging ragged breaths, fighting to draw air into his lungs, he saw the sword separate itself from the eyes he'd encountered. As he calmed down, his breathing returning to normal, he watched a hooded form detach itself from the back of the absolute largest horse he'd ever encountered and start moving towards him.

The sword was attached to the hooded being, of course, and didn't waver from the point it had previously punctured.

The sword stopped only inches from him.

"Who are you, and what are you doing in my father's forest?"

took the letter and folded it carefully. She used a small

Hudson blinked.

"You're a girl!"

Wrong answer. The tip of the razor sharp blade navigated from his chest to point at his neck.

"I meant...wait! Don't, don't do anything rash, now," he said, pushing himself as far back into the tree as he could manage. "I just mean…you don't…you're…"

"She's got her hood on and you can't see her face," a voice supplied from behind her.

The figure whipped her head around, glaring at whomever had spoken.

The blade didn't move.

She looked back toward Hudson, and now her hood was further back on her head. He could see shining brunette locks now, one particular lock being particularly darling—and suitably annoying, he was sure—hanging between her eyes.

Her eyes were dark, like her hair. Her lips full, like her mother's.

"Oh my Gods, you're Hilda."

And Hudson's world mercifully went black.

"That was completely your fault," Hilda told Hadley as she maneuvered the unconscious man onto the back of her horse. "You scared him by talking."

Hadley showed no sign of remorse. "You scared him by being you," he replied.

He was smirking. Hilda couldn't tell by looking at

amount of wax and took the large signet ring from

him because he was a horse, but he was. She knew he was.

"Just because my father is one of the first immortals, and my mother happens to be like the only human to ever have a child by him even though a million others have tried does not make me someone to be afraid of."

"No. It's just the omen that surrounds you that's frightening."

Having a prophet announce that the first child born of a mortal mother and an immortal father would be the child to end the world was kind of frightening.

She'd give him that.

But they didn't say *when* she would end the world, now did they? Nope. It could be millions of years from now! Her father could only remember the last few thousand. So who knew how long they would inhabit this place? Maybe she'd end the world by moving everyone somewhere else.

It could happen.

"Whatever," she finally replied, making sure that the unconscious man was evenly balanced on Hadley's back. "Let's get out of here. I want to talk to this guy some more."

"Maybe this time without the weapon," Hadley suggested.

Maybe. Hilda would think on it.

her thin and withered fingers to press in Joseph's

monogram. He would know it was from her, because

he had given her the ring when he promised to marry

I is for...ivy

*I*vy grew across the walls and the doors, sealing the palace shut, forbidding entrance to all. No one dare enter, even if they could. Having grown for decades, the plants were thick, nearing two feet in places. A tangle of life dedicated to keeping everything out.

Except Isabelle.

<!-- * * * -->

Her father openly laughed at her idea while her mother merely snorted, then kept an even face.

"You're going to what?" He actually redefined 'guffaw' for Isabelle, from something jovial and fun to something snide and cruel. "You haven't got a chance."

her. When he promised to love her forever, and never

Isabelle watched her mother lose her composure, but at least she put her hand in front of her grin, and tried to hold her body still while laughter shook her.

Thank goodness for small favors.

Looking back at her father, she could feel defeat clawing at her shoulders. Straightening them, she shook it off. She was going to do this whether he liked it or not.

"Just give me what's owed me," she said in a voice that was supposed to sound commanding.

It squeaked. She had to admit it, even to herself.

He only laughed harder.

So she left them, not defeated, but definitely with a renewed awareness of how difficult this was about to be. Climbing the stairs, she went to one of the two rooms on the second floor.

Isabelle wanted to call it her own, but it wasn't. Not really.

Her parents had the other room. This was more like the place where Isabelle slept when company wasn't visiting.

She wasn't some Cinderella case. Her parents weren't dead (obviously—she'd just been talking to them), they hadn't left her to some shitty life.

They just didn't understand her.

Isabella craved adventure. And she worked hard for her father at his business, and she didn't think it was unreasonable to expect at least a modest wage. She wasn't asking for what a real employee would earn, just a portion of it.

hurt her. When he should have protected her from

Now it was obvious he considered her free labor. Well, his free labor was about to set herself free.

<!-- * * * -->

She packed light. She didn't have much she could consider her own anyway, only what she'd been given as gifts, or earned in trade from neighbors.

An extra dress, a change of shirt and pants, a necklace that had been a gift from a young girl she'd taught to read, and a small knife in a hard leather sheaf.

Okay, so her father would have definitely not approved of the last item. But she'd come by it honestly, even if he wouldn't have seen it that way.

She left at the last moment before dawn, when her father would be enjoying the deep sleep of a drunkard, and her mother would have fallen asleep after hours of trying to keep her father out of trouble.

Isabelle didn't leave a note. It wasn't worth it. They would know where she'd gone, and they would laugh about it at first, and then regret the loss of the hardest working member of her family, and then...

Well, they wouldn't forget her. Isabelle would make sure of that.

<!-- * * * -->

The walls were taller than Isabelle expected. No one approached the castle anymore, they merely told

those who accused her of such foul deeds...

stories, but usually tales grew taller with time.

Not nearly as tall as the reality, apparently.

But she was pretty sure the way wasn't over. She was the only one who thought so, the only one who had ever breathed the possibility. Everyone else figured it was so thick, why not just climb?

Isabelle started walking. You didn't know a thing until you studied it, so she walked.

There was no way to tell gate from wall. The entire thing may very well have been wall from what you could tell while looking at it.

Then again, no one knew like Isabelle that appearances were deceiving. So she walked again. She stopped occasionally, taking her knife and taking a crack at some of the vines, but it was hard and long work. Her blade would dull far before she was able to clear the castle walls.

And when she finally realized that visual inspection wasn't going to reveal any weaknesses, it was nightfall.

Isabelle was exhausted. She pulled her extra clothing out of her pack and put it all on. She didn't have any way to create a fire or other way to keep herself warm; layers it was. Curling her body into a ball and huddling into a small crevice she cut into the ivy, Isabelle tried to sleep.

¶ Mathilda hurled the ring as hard as she could

She managed an entire three hours, judging by the position of the moon, before she was woken by the light.

It surrounded her, a glow brighter than the moonlight and a different shade. It was positively green, actually. Isabelle crawled from her cave, still dressed in three layers of clothing, marveling at the scene before her.

Why had no one noticed this before? What was this light, and where did it come from?

It took her a moment to realize that part of the glow was coming from her.

She pushed her sleeve up her arm and saw a light pulsing from her skin. It was a vine of ivy that wound from the back of her hand, around her wrist, and up under her clothing.

She stripped off the long sleeved shirt she wore over the dress, then the dress, then the extra pants. Isabelle followed the light, almost like a tattoo, that wound up her arm, across her shoulders and back, and down the sides of her legs.

It was everywhere. It did not rub off. It was glowing green, just like the ivy on the castle walls.

"I knew it," she whispered to herself. "I knew it!" redressing quickly and leaving her pack, she started walking around the castle again as quickly as she could. When she saw the glow on her skin fading, she turned around and ran the other direction. It should have been hard to see where she was going, but her skin was

into the fire, remembering now that Joseph had not

acting like a lantern. Her footing wasn't completely sure, but she managed not to fall and twist any limbs.

It wasn't long before the light started fading again, and she doubled back.

She'd blasted right by it the first time. Where the the light pulsed through the ivy, and the light on her skin responded.

She reached out, and the ivy vines parted for her hand.

She felt the edge of a gate.

She'd found it.

Isabelle Hedera took the first steps into the ivy castle in five hundred years.

managed to protect her. He had let them convict her of

his murder, when he obviously had not died. He could

not die. Her love kept him alive.

J is for...jewelry

A necklace, a bracelet and a ring. Separately they were beautiful, stunning pieces of jewelry. Women over the ages fought over them, jealous of any who were enhanced by the pieces.

But together...together they were something else entirely.

<!-- * * * -->

"Daddy!"

A smile grew on Jason's face. His daughter was home! He had such a surprise for her, and his anticipation of her happiness was almost more than his satisfaction that he had managed this feat in the first place.

¶ Panting, Mathilda pressed her hands against her

"Here, in the library," he called back. He quickly set the three boxes on top of his impeccably neat desk, arranging them in a small tower of gifts, and then relaxed into his chair, folding his hands on the mound of his stomach.

"Daddy, I'm home!"

He watched her rush across the room, and raising his arms he was enveloped in the sweetest of hugs. Gently he patted her on the back, then released her as she raised up to stare at the small tower on his desk.

"Welcome home, Jane."

"Is that for me?" She was pointing at the gorgeous and expertly inlaid wooden boxes, each one with a different colored ribbon.

Jason nodded. "Your wedding gift," he said, trying to hold back his smile. "Open it."

Jane squealed in excitement, grabbing all three boxes and sitting in the large chair opposite his desk.

She chose the smallest box first. The ribbon slid through the bow he had made. One moment it was an extravagant piece of artwork, the next simply a pretty piece of silk draped across his daughter's lap.

When she lifted the lid it was as if the box was lit from inside. His daughter's face was painted with colorful light. Blues and greens danced across her face, matching her eyes.

"Daddy," she said, looking up excitedly. "Is this what I think it is?"

Jason nodded. "It is. Go ahead, open the next."

Another ribbon creation fell to pieces, and a

skirts, smoothing their surface where they had been

bracelet was revealed. A shining, shimmering sea of stones, throwing yellow and amber lights when the sun hit its jewels. Beautiful beyond all imagining, and meant to take one's breath away.

Which, of course, it did. Jane gasped. Holding the box this way and that in the light, she watched the colors shine on the walls of her father's office.

"Go on. Open the last one."

Jane was past the gentle, elegant presentation. Frantically she pulled at the ribbon on the last box and was rewarded. The last box contained the necklace that bathed her face in red light, as if a fire approached and she was about to be consumed.

"Daddy," Jane breathed, "these are…"

She couldn't finish her sentence, but Jason knew what she meant.

"They are," he confirmed.

"But they've never been seen in the same place since they were created. How did you…"

Jason smiled. "I've been working towards this since you were a baby. Your mother had the bracelet, from her father. Something borrowed."

"And the ring, something blue," she reminded him.

"Yes. I discovered it was up for sale just recently. Got it for a steal, as the previous owner did not know its true worth."

"How could they not?" Jane picked up the ring box again, admiring its beauty. "Even on its own it was said to be the most beautiful and priceless ring ever seen. Queens wore this ring, Daddy!"

ruffled from her little outburst. Of course her love kept

"And the necklace...well, let's just say you're worth it."

Jane set the boxes back on her father's desk and ran around to give him a giant hug.

He squeezed back gently, then set his daughter back on her feet. "Try them on," he suggested.

She walked back to the chair, and took the necklace out first.

"No, start with the ring."

So she did, sitting back down in the large, comfortable chair. He handed the small ring box back over to his daughter, and she accepted it with appropriate reverence.

"Shall I put it on for you," he asked her, but she shook her head. "No, the next man to put a ring on me will be my husband."

Disappointed but understanding, Jason nodded.

The ring, which had never been re-sized for any of its owners, slid on her finger, fitting perfectly.

It always did.

"Oh, Daddy..."

Jason smiled. It took a lot to render his daughter speechless.

"Now the bracelet," he instructed. She reached for that box herself, opening it and pulling out the silver bangle that was adorned with jewels, so beautiful it took one's breath away.

"Amazing. Simply amazing."

"Last but not least," Jane said in a shaking voice as she reached for the necklace. She examined the clasp

him alive. And he would write her when he read her

for a moment, deciding how it worked and whether she would be able to manage it herself. After a moment, she raised both hands behind her neck, fiddled with her hair, and finally, brought her hands down to her side.

It was done. Jason thought she looked beautiful.

It was just too bad she would never be his Jane again.

He watched as Jane's face twisted. She felt the pain first, and confusion followed swiftly.

"Daddy?"

Her voice was that of a child, sounding so much like his little girl when she'd run outside and scraped up a knee, but he steeled himself against it.

He made himself watch her transformation from beautiful, elegant girl to transparent, smokeless fire. He could see through her, see the nearly invisible chains that now connected the only solid parts about her anymore—the necklace, bracelet and ring were strung together with metal that made no sound.

The only thing Jason could hear was the sound of his own fortune; it was about to multiply exponentially, practically overnight.

Jane's voice was no longer childlike. It was low, and gravely—a voice as old as the jewelry she was wearing.

"You have made me whole, master. What do you wish? Ask and it shall be yours."

Jason smiled. He had lost his daughter, but he was about to gain so much more.

letter, because she had poured all of her love for him

into it. He would see that, and know she was sorry. He

K is for ...knife

*W*hatchya doin'?"

Katrina scowled. "That's a pretty lousy question to ask in the middle of a fight," she replied as she took a swing at one of her attackers, slicing his throat and spinning to catch another behind the knee, ducking the broadsword aimed at her neck.

He pressed his back against hers, protecting her weak spot.

If she had one.

"I don't know, it seemed like a valid question," he punctuated his point by lunging forward to puncture an attacker's chest, then heart. "You know, an attractive girl like you," *slice*, "coming to a place like this," *stab*, "in a dress."

would write to her, and tell her he loved her, and he

Katrina felt her forehead furrowing deeper. "It's a ceremonial gown," she said with gritted teeth as she managed to take down the last attacker in the inept first group of assassins. "This is my palace. I belong here."

Unlike you, was left unsaid.

"They just keep coming," she panted as another wave approached. "Where have they all come from?".

"I'm not sure, but it probably doesn't matter. We're in trouble. Don't you have a bodyguard or something? Someone to save you when things like this happen?"

Katrina watched the men coming toward her. They were creeping now, not rushing as the previous group had done. She did not recognize the identical uniforms they wore: red robes, cinched at the waist with rope, and split between the legs creating a jumper of sorts. They had similar faces, long, with short cropped hair. They didn't look angry, only determined.

They were here for her, Katarina, Honored Guardian of the Blade, and her charge, the item she was sworn to protect. The Kissing Knife.

But they had killed her guards, the men who surrounded her so she could protect the blade. Her guards lay on the ground around her, covered by the bodies of the first wave of attackers. The ones who had come to see how strong her defenses were, and to see if they even needed to risk their best warriors to retrieve the blade.

They had, but not to defeat her guards.

Katrina was the threat. She knew it, and now they did, too.

would never hurt her. He would forgive her.

"Who are you?"

He had appeared, dropped in from above her and landed at her side. Casual, deadly, but apparently on her side.

Katrina had not bothered to question before, as he was helping her. Now, as her attackers surrounded them, it seemed odd not to know before they either killed more or died themselves.

"I'm Kale," he answered. "I'm very pleased to meet you, Mistress."

He knew the proper way to address her, which meant he was from around here. That was good.

"Ditto. So, do you think you can help me out of here?" The attackers were coming closer. They didn't have much time, and Katrina raised her sword, preparing for the worst.

"Probably," Kale replied. "It is sort of why I came by."

The Kissing Knife, settled up on its pedestal, was within Katrina's grasp, but Kale snatched it first. "After you?"

And it was only then that Katrina saw the rope ladder hanging behind the blade's pedestal.

<!-- * * * -->

His airship pulled them from the palace, Katrina in her ceremonial gowns, Kale with one arm on the ladder and one arm around her. They were being winched up to safety as the ship took off away from her palace.

¶ Patting down the hairs that never stayed put in

It was here that she could see the full nature of the danger she had been in.

Her palace was under attack.

Her city.

Her blade.

Finally they were inside, and Kale rushed off to a console to push some buttons while Katrina pressed herself against a window, staring down at the ground.

Priests, ministers, shopkeepers…they were laying in the streets, surrounded by black circles of blood. The men who had rushed the Chambers of the Blade were everywhere.

"What is happening?"

Katrina whispered it to herself, but Kale was back at her side. "I don't know. Here," he handed her the blade that she was born to protect. "You'll probably want that later."

She looked down at it, a simple, relatively unadorned dagger with a less than memorable name. But it required an Honored Guardian, a set of guards simply while it lay in its chambers, and countless numbers of priests, holy men, etc.

"I don't know," she replied quietly, "it doesn't seem like much right now, does it? Certainly not worth all this," she added, gesturing down to the bloody massacre below.

"Yeah, maybe not. But still. It's your job to protect it. And my job to protect you."

She looked at the man who called himself Kale. "What, you're not just a right place, right time kind of

the bun that Joseph favored, Mathilda stood from her

guy?"

She was joking.

Kale was not.

"Nope."

Katrina blinked.

"Mistress, Honored Guardian of the Kissing Knife, allow me to properly introduce myself. I am Kale, Honored Guardian of the Honored Guardian of the Kissing Knife."

She blinked again. "You're kidding, right? That's a little excessive."

"But today, necessary. There's always been one of me. You ladies just never know about us."

"Why is that, again?"

"In case of days like today, when the horde attacks, we are not a target, we are a secret weapon, coming to defend you, when possible, and the blade when not."

"So if I'd already been dead you would have simply gone for the knife?"

"Yep."

Katrina shuddered as she looked back outside. They had picked up speed, and now were quite far from her palace. "Nice to know I'm so disposable."

"You're not, you know," he said gently from behind her. "Without you, there would be no way to avenge your household. Your family."

He was talking of the legend. The reason they protected the blade. The set of words she'd been practically marinated in since she was born so she would protect the Kissing Knife with her life when the

secretary and walked to her door. It was tall, made

time came.

As she had.

Katrina sighed. "I suppose you're right. So are you ready?"

"Never been more," Kale replied.

And he sounded just as unenthusiastic as Katrina felt.

of heavy wood, and reinforced with steel. There was

a small window that opened only from the outside,

and a small knocker for her to use so she did not need

$\mathscr{L}$ is for ...lies

imitless.   Possibilities,   potential, adventures.
          Lies.
Lorelei was most familiar with the latter, unfortunately.

She was always on the delivery side.

She couldn't help it. She blamed it on her upbringing. Lies kept you safe when she was growing up. If you lied, if you told people what they wanted to hear, you didn't get hit.

Or locked in your room for the weekend.

Or worse.

And when you lived your entire childhood telling falsehoods simply to survive, was it really any wonder that now, as an adult, Lorelei couldn't help but continue

to damage her delicate hands calling for assistance.

her bad habits?

<!-- * * * -->

Lorelei was in a bad spot.

"You told me you would have it done."

"And I will! I still have a few hours. I can still get it done, I promise!"

"Your time is almost over. It should have been done by now."

"No, it'll totally be done, in plenty of time. Before the deadline."

"You know what it is to promise me?"

Lorelei nodded her head furiously. "No, I totally know. I take this so seriously, like a heart attack."

The very large man facing her, intimidating her, scowled. "Perhaps a poor choice of words."

He left as quietly as he'd entered, and through the same door.

Lorelei deflated.

"I am so screwed," she said to the empty room, and it was the first truthful thing she'd said all day.

It had started innocently enough. She made her boss a promise that she would be able to accomplish a task by a deadline for one of his clients.

It didn't escape her that she was often making promises she couldn't really make good on.

How was the progress? Fine. Was she on schedule? Absolutely. Did she need an extension? No, Lorelei had come in the past weekend and had made great progress,

Someone was waiting on her today, as always, and

and now was just a breath away from completion.

It also didn't escape her that she was learning to believe her own bullshit. There was no other way to explain why she had gone out drinking with friends every night for the past week.

The last week she had for the project.

Yeah, she was screwed.

<!-- * * * -->

Two hours left. Lorelei was packing. She had gone into work shortly after her visitor had left her home, packaged everything up as nicely as she could, hoping almost against hope that someone would see it and think she'd managed to do what she knew was impossible.

It might buy her some time.

She didn't think about the fact that her home was probably being watched. No, that didn't cross her mind as she spun around her apartment in a frenzy, deciding what she would take now, and what she would try to send someone for later.

Her heart pounded through her chest, beating so hard she could feel it in the palms of her hands.

One bag packed, clothing and such, plus another bag full of necessities like cash, her computer, and the like. Perhaps she could move to another state and start over. Pick a new name; Lorelei was getting worn out. She had only used it a year, but still.

He would be looking for Lorelei Lake. Not...

opened the window immediately.

What other name would be good? Lilly? Lilac? Lucy? Leta?

Still spinning names through her head, she didn't notice the sound of her front door opening until it was too late.

<!-- * * * -->

"You know how our organization values honesty," a voice Lorelei didn't recognize said, only slightly muffled by the canvas bag that was hung loosely over her head.

She was breathing in hot, scared air, and was long past the worry that she would end up suffocating, despite the breathable fabric.

In fact, at this point she was almost hoping for suffocation. Why couldn't they have chosen a plastic bag, anyway? Wasn't that how it used to be done?

"And you have lied, Ms. Lake. Not only to me, but to the boss himself."

Lorelei tried not to wet herself.

"Beyond that, you are incompetent."

He droned on, listing the ways she had failed, building up an impressive monologue.

Lorelei wondered if death would hurt. She'd always thought it would be horrible to die the way her father had, choking on a pool of his own vomit. Or like her mother, at the hands of an angry step-father who believed she was cheating on him.

It had probably been the only truth her mother had

¶ "Please put this in today's post, Sir," she said softly

ever told, when she denied it.

"Well? Don't you have anything to say for yourself?"

She could only whimper. What could she say? That there had never been any hope of anyone getting the task done on time, much less by her? With her track record? Why had they trusted her with something so important anyway? It had really been their own fault, this mess. She should be held blameless in this accusation.

Not that they would appreciate hearing that.

They needed someone to blame.

So their own hides would be safe.

From him.

"No?"

Lorelei managed to shake her head.

The only response she could manage.

The only honest one.

There was nothing to say. It probably was about time she should pay for her lies.

"Fine, then."

The curtain came down on Lorelei's last lie.

in a voice that was worn from years of near-constant

screaming, tears, and curses.

M is for...marriage

erritt, would you please do the honor of marrying me?"

Merritt stopped in her tracks. She had been leaving the room after visiting her best friend, but now she was frozen.

No way. No way he had just asked her that. Wasn't possible. She'd been hearing things.

"I know this might come as a shock to you. It must. But please, Merritt...will you do this for me? Before..."

"Shht," she said, silencing him. "Mark, just shut up." She cringed when that came out of her mouth, but she didn't regret it. She didn't want to hear any more. Didn't want to think about it.

"It's not nice to talk to a dying man like that, you know," he replied quietly.

¶ "Yes, Mistress," the deep voice replied, and took

Merritt finally turned. She hated seeing him like this. Her strong, proud friend reduced to a withering sack of bones in a hospital bed. Sterility all around him, with a cloud of death suffocating the room.

His face was no longer handsome, his hair missing in patches. But she could still see her friend.

"Sorry," Merritt managed. "But come on. You don't need to worry about stuff like that right now. You need to concentrate on getting better," she choked out on a sob. "I've got to go."

And this time she made it out of the room. She made it only a few steps before she broke out into a run, hearing Mark's voice call her name from the door she'd left open.

She ran faster, pushing past a nurse, and upon finally reaching the elevators, frantically hitting the buttons, hoping that sheer force of will would bring the car faster.

She lunged through the doors as soon as they opened, knocking a guy in a suit back into the car as he tried to exit.

Merritt pressed her face into the corner, the cool metal of the walls helping calm her down. What was her friend thinking? Marriage? Now? He was on the verge of death, infected with a cancer that they hadn't been able to beat.

She felt her balled fist smash against the elevator car's wall, and she repeated it until the pain in her hand overwhelmed the pain in her heart.

When she felt a hand on her shoulder, she nearly

the letter gently from her fingers. She could not see the

took that fist and smashed it against the head of the person in the car with her.

Luckily, he ducked.

"Whoa, there, calm down!" His hands were up in the air, surrendering. "Are you okay? I just wanted to see if you were okay."

Merritt found herself panting, breathing hard, pressed against the back wall. Was she okay? Not really. Her best friend was suggesting they get married on his deathbed. There really wasn't anything okay about that.

"I'm fine," she lied, slowing her breathing and managing to get a grip. "Sorry. I didn't mean to hit you."

"Fortunately, I have fast reflexes. What's going on? Did you get some bad news down on fifty-two?"

Of course she'd gotten bad news. What other kind of news was there on sub-level fifty-two of the Unified Underground Hospital Network? It's where the most severe cases went. The last stop. The furthest to travel for the families that insisted on supporting their practically dead fathers, mothers, sisters, brothers, cousins...or best friends.

"I'm fine."

He didn't believe her, and it showed on his face. "Right. Well, where are you headed? I can at least get you to your floor."

"I'm going to the surface," she said without thinking. Yes. That's where she needed to be. In the gardens, where it was quiet. Peaceful.

person guarding her against the evil that was outside,

"Um...are you sure? I was headed up to Surface 15, there's a real nice little place up there where we could get a drink. I know the owner, we'll get a table with good views."

Merritt stared at the stranger. What was this? People weren't just nice, there was always a motive. Mark and she had lived by that rule their whole lives. It was just them together, they couldn't trust anyone else. No one would look out for them like they would look out for each other.

Which was why it was going to be so damn lonely without him.

"Fine, yeah. That sounds good." Apparently she was in a mood to live dangerously. The surface wasn't dangerous, but the surface levels were.

Especially for someone like her.

"Good!" He took out his card and swiped it in the panel, pushing the appropriate code on the keypad, and the elevator took off.

Merritt never liked elevators. She could feel them moving even when no one else could, and she always felt like she was moving in the wrong direction.

"So you've got someone sick down there?"

"Dying," she corrected automatically. "He wants me to marry him."

"Really? Wow, that's some off timing."

"Tell me about it. We're friends. Best friends. He doesn't need to be worrying about this now. He needs to fight."

"Fight what?"

but she took comfort from his voice.

"Some kind of cancer they won't cure," she replied automatically before correcting herself. "Can't cure, I mean."

"Well, I'm really sorry to hear that."

He actually sounded concerned, too. It felt good to have someone to talk to that was a little removed from the situation.

Their elevator arrived, and Merritt stepped off first. She'd never spent a lot of time in the surface levels. They seemed artificial, and entirely too clean. She liked being able to get a little dirty, to play in the gardens, pick weeds. It made her feel like she was home.

Inside just felt like a prison.

"Two, please," her companion said to the man standing beside the door of the cafe bar thing they were about to enter. "Can we get a table near the windows?"

She noticed him flashing his card to the other guy, and wondered to herself if it would be worth stealing.

But she was tired. She was tired of fighting to live. Maybe it would be worth getting married, just so she could breathe a little easier before going to bed at night. Not having to worry about where the next meal would come from.

They were seated, and two glasses were set on their table. He didn't ask what they wanted, just pushed a few buttons, waved his card, and they were filled with something that smelled much like the flowers she'd seen outside about a month ago, and had about the same color.

"What's this?"

¶ She knew the man protecting her would deliver her

"Oh, I hope you don't mind. It's my favorite, something I made up once that just kind of stuck around, you know?"

She knew. Lots of things just kind of showed up and stuck around. You grew attached to them, and then couldn't imagine life without them.

"Want to tell me about your friend?"

Merritt sighed. She did. She desperately did. But still, she held her tongue. "Not now."

Her companion nodded. "Well, I'm Terrik," he said, holding out his hand. "I know formalities like this seem a little silly after you've already tried to deck me, but..."

He was smiling at her. Merritt looked at his face for any sign of pretense, but there wasn't. He was simply smiling.

She tried returning it, and shook his hand.

"Wow, it's been a while for you?"

"What do you mean?"

"Smiling. Yours is kind of rusty."

This time her smile was genuine. "I suppose so. I haven't had much to smile about since Mark got sick."

"How sick is he?"

Merritt's face grew dark. "Only a few days. They're just making him comfortable. The cancer...it's taken over his heart."

Terrik reached over to take Merritt's hand. When she raised her gaze to his, he raised his glass.

"To Mark," he said quietly.

Merritt smiled, raised her glass as well, then drank

letter, and Joseph would receive it and forgive her. The

until the glass was empty.

"So, what are you going to do?"

Marrying Mark...that would put her in a whole different class. She'd spent her life an orphan, without family, the worst offense in the world she lived in. No one was willing to claim her, so she lived on the surface, in the slums. She watched the towers, hating what they represented, hating that she couldn't have it. At some point she had stopped wanting to be part of them and started actively avoiding things that could have gotten her in.

Marriage would change her status. A widow was an honored woman in her world. No, it didn't make sense that a widow would have honor where an orphan would not, but widows never stayed unwed long. Men would swarm to their sides, beg to help them rebuild their familes. There would be assistance from the government, and a place to stay.

A warm bed, away from the rains and the snowstorms that created such lush landscapes for the towers to view from a distance.

"I don't know," Merritt replied. "I just don't know."

thought of receiving a letter from her beloved buoyed

her spirits even as they sank. Sometimes she didn't

N is for...nefarious

*I*t was a brave, new world. There were things to be discovered, creatures to be cataloged, people to study.

Nice couldn't wait.

She was eager to dissect something this week. Today would be the perfect opportunity.

They had landed on N56 just a few weeks before, long enough to get the laboratories built out of something other than canvas, and move all the equipment out of storage on the ship and into the new labs. The security forces were organized and arranged, with a perimeter established out of the newest and best technologies.

There were a few colonists, but not many. Mostly just the rabble they'd recruited at the last minute off

understand how she could be so sad while she was so

the streets, people to do manual labor in exchange for a new life.

They had another job, of course, but only Nice knew what that was going to be.

During the construction period, Nice had spent her time back on the ship, studying the planet from afar. There were several very interesting native species of large cats that she could identify, along with the rest of the animals on the planet that she could not. She was less interested in the flora, although she did realize that it could perhaps be the more aggressive of the two.

Using the ship's capabilities, she was able to transport some of the more common plants in their area to her lab on board. They seemed harmless enough, and edible too. She added them to the list of possible food sources if their own didn't take to the nutrients provided in this foreign soil.

Finally, she was ready for her real work. The skills that made her the perfect choice—the only choice, really—for the first team. Other scientists would follow, and then she'd be forced to do things their way. The slow, humane way.

It disgusted her. They would waste so much time.

Which was why it was critical that she accomplish as much as possible in the three months she was allotted before the second ship arrived.

That one would be full of colonists. A massive crowd ready to destroy another planet like they'd destroyed her own. Full of people who would be missed, all with litigators back home ready to argue their way into her

eager for Joseph's reply. Perhaps she was just tired.

pockets.

Nice shuddered. Disgusting little rats.

She was ready to get to work now, though.

It was time.

<!-- * * * -->

"Norm, would you bring that specimen over here, please?"

Norm did as he was asked. The AGG, or anti-grav gurney, had been difficult to maneuver at first, but he'd quickly become skilled.

It was important to do your job right when working with a sadist.

"Here you go, Miss," he replied. Never by her first name, never ever "Ma'am". "Doctor" probably would have been okay, but once he'd landed on something that didn't offend her, he was reluctant to change.

He grabbed the opposite end of the sheet, lifting with her to transfer the sedated, but not unconscious, body over to the surgical table.

"Perfect. Now, I need my usual tools. Please bring them over."

While she did a surface examination, he hurried—but didn't run, accidents happened when you ran—to get her instruments. She kept them in a black leather bag, something he was pretty sure had been banned quite some time ago on Earth. But here...well, she could very well have gotten it manufactured here. He had seen a lot of animals come in and out of her lab,

¶ She would take a nap, she decided. A rest never

and some had black hides.

"Thank you," she said when he set her bag down on the usual table. There was a button on top next to the clasp that read her fingerprint—not that anyone in their right mind would dare try to open any of her things without her permission. Not anyone who knew what she was doing in here.

Which meant Norm did not touch unless asked to touch.

They thought the people they'd gathered from the street were stupid, and granted, probably quite a few of them were. Over the course of the trip they had been fattened up, given good food and warm places to sleep, and they'd grown strong. They knew they were being brought as basically slave labor, but after living so long in squalor, many didn't care. Some figured that they would learn a new skill and when the need came, fill those job positions. Others thought that they'd be forgotten as soon as the regular colonists showed up, and they could go back to begging, if that was their preferred method of living out their lives.

Some, like Norm, knew that they probably would be able to learn enough about survival here in the first few months that when the second, or even third wave of colonists arrived, they could escape in the confusion and go and build their own lives. Away from the crowds that ignored them, away from the cities that scared them.

Unfortunately—or maybe fortunately, depending on how you looked at it—Norm had been assigned

failed to revive her when she was confused.

to work with the scientist Nice. At the very least, he certainly would learn a lot.

He quietly watched Nice take her scalpel to the chest of the first gen colonist. He watched the man's eyes plead for him to intercede, staring at both of them in horror. The man's eyes were screaming for him, bulging, frantic.

Norm desperately hoped Nice didn't find a way to audibly animate the eyes of the men and women she examined. He hoped she never explained what she was looking for, and more than anything else, he feared she would run out of bodies before the rest of the colonists arrived.

¶ Mathilda didn't notice the smell of mildew coming

from the mattress, or the small insects that milled

O is for...only

*O*nly one option remained. Olive didn't want to go that route, but there really was nothing else to do. Any other path would lead to ruin, and that she could not afford.

Ruin was something none of them could afford.

Olive looked over at the cots that filled the room. They were filled with people, some cots holding two children or a mother and child.

It was what was left of her family, her kingdom. The people who had relied on her, followed her through more than she could ever have dreamed to ask of them, and now were suffering the fate they had been trying to escape.

Capture, the loss of their freedom. Freedom was the most important thing to her, to everyone following

around on her pillow when she lay down her head.

her. Being forced to stay inside, against their will, it was painful. Already they had lost three young men to a condition known to them as Flightless. Like birds caught and forced to live in the giant aviaries Oren's people created for their own pleasure, their young men who had known nothing but absolute freedom of personal choice succumbed quickly to depression, then death by consuming the five poisonous dried berries each of them carried on their person.

Most had been able to resist, reassured by Olive's promises that they would certainly be released soon.

Still, not all shared her confidence.

Now Olive, who was the leader of these fiercely independent people, was facing the most distasteful prison of all.

Marriage.

Commitment was one thing. Many of her people committed themselves to each other for their entire lives, and others for shorter, but no less meaningful times.

Marriage was something completely different.

It was an unbreakable institution for Oren's people. Women, once married, were not allowed to leave their husband's home. It was said that the women were kept in unspeakable luxury, treasured, and treated to everything their hearts desired, but for Olive...

The one thing she wanted, needed, was freedom. And that was something married women did not have.

"You can't do this. You can't give yourself up for us."

Instead, she smoothed her skirts again, and pulled the

Olive looked over at her best friend and smiled. "I have to do this. I can't let them," she gestured to the young adults in the group, "live like this."

"It's a prison, no matter what the result, Olive. Either you live in marriage and we live with the knowledge what you've given up for us, or we all join you in the situation together."

Olive shook her head. "The little ones, the babies, they would grow into the situation. And the elders, they would die soon anyway, and would not have to live long with the pain. But you...the rest of them...I can not condemn everyone to death like that."

"But you would condemn yourself?"

"To set everyone free? Yes. They would find a new leader. You, most likely. And you could lead them away from this, to somewhere that they could never find you again."

"There may not be many places like that left."

"Well you could find it if there is one."

Olive's friend sighed, and Olive wrapped an arm around her. "I need to do this now," she told her. "So that the next morning our people wake to is a free one."

She gave her friend another squeeze, then walked to the doorway. There were no cots next to the door. They had all kept as far away from it as possible. It represented their prison, that they were being kept there against their will.

There was a panel beside the door, and Olive had been told that when she was ready to wed Oren, all she needed to do was press the button, and they would be

quilt she'd made for her wedding bed up to her chin.

freed.

So Olive pressed the button.

The door was opened immediately, and she wasn't given the chance to even whisper a prayer of protection. She felt her friend's eyes on her as she left, and before the door was shut behind her, Olive was able to see her friend for the last time.

The door latched behind her, and Olive tried to contain her fear. The guard looked so foreign to her, wearing constricting clothing and carrying weapons meant not for food but for people. She followed the man who said nothing to her, just allowed her to follow him through the dark hallways.

The point at which she was asked to get into a conveyance that moved under its own power was the point at which Olive nearly refused to go any further. She had never gone anywhere that she couldn't get on her own two feet before, not even to the prison she had just left.

But she reminded herself of her obligation to the people she had left behind. She got into the car, and closed her eyes tightly against the movement. Just when she decided that she could no longer endure the ride and not get sick, the movement stopped.

Thankfully.

And she was led out again, and into a very large building settled between equally large buildings.

Finally, she was presented to Oren.

And she recognized him.

"You," she said on a gasp, immediately before

¶   Sleep claimed her quickly, and the room was silent

collapsing to the ground, unconscious.

<!-- * * * -->

Oren sighed. He had hoped Olive would be a little stronger when she faced him. He had so wanted to talk with her, to tell her about his life since they had been separated five years before. He wanted to share how much he'd missed her, to explain why he'd never returned to their home.

He wanted to apologize for forcing her hand in this manner, but promise her that whatever she wanted was hers. Of course, he might not share that she only needed to ask for her freedom for him to be obliged to give it to her. He knew she would have ideas about what she was to expect, and that she wouldn't ask for her freedom thinking that she would never receive it.

He instructed his guards to move her to his chambers. They would have enough time to talk about it when she woke.

When they were married.

but for the crackles and snaps from the fireplace.

<!-- * * * -->

$\mathcal{P}$ is for...pencil

*H*ave you ever had a magic pencil? Paige did. And the way she figured it, when she was around nine or so, no one else really could have made as good use of it as she did.

Pencil, Paige. They were meant for each other.

The pencil had been a gift from her grandmother when she started her third year of school. Paige thought it very strange for her grandmother to give her such a gift in celebration.

It was school. She could buy a thousand pencils in the aisles of the nearest department store, and a hundred pencil cases to hold them.

Grandmother's pencil was ordinary, and packaged in a purple velvet box with spring hinges. It was new, unsharpened. Unused

¶ Bernard watched through the small window as the

"What is this?" Paige tried really hard not to sound ungrateful, just curious.

"It's a pencil," her grandmother said with a smile.

Paige hated it when her grandma tried to be silly.

"I *know* it's a pencil, Grandma. But why is it in such a pretty box? It's just a regular pencil." *And it doesn't even have sparkles or magical rainbow-colored ponies all over it*, but Paige didn't say that out loud.

"How do you know it's regular? You haven't tried using it yet!"

And that was all the information she got, as her grandmother was called to the kitchen by Paige's mother.

She didn't think much about it at the time, she simply put the pencil away.

<!-- * * * -->

When she finally got her gift out, the school year was nearly over. All the girls in the class came back from Easter with stories about their wonderful gifts, and new pet bunnies and chicks, and Paige had nothing. Her father had lost his job, her mother just found out she was pregnant, and on Easter Sunday her grandmother had died in church of a heart attack.

Paige's life was completely ruined, and all her friends could talk about were bunnies.

With no new toys, or new dresses, or pet bunnies, Paige was sent to the school counselor for punching Bettie Sue after she said Paige couldn't be friends with

murderer on the other side of the door lay down as

any of the girls anymore because she hadn't got some sort of pet for Easter, not even a guinea pig.

"Paige, I hear you've been having some hard times at home."

Paige sat still on her chair, hands in her lap. She was pinching herself in an effort not to cry, refusing to look at Mr. Pearson, the school counselor.

"You know you can't take your anger out on the other girls, right?"

Paige nodded sullenly.

"Now, what you need is a way to express your feelings without using your fists."

Silence.

"Do you like to read?"

Paige practiced the fine art of shrugging.

"Write, maybe?"

She repeated the exercise, letting her shoulders rise and fall dramatically

Mr. Pearson pulled open a drawer in his big, ugly, wood-topped metal desk. Paige shuddered at the shriek it made, but otherwise kept staring at the only thing on Mr. Pearson's desk that was uglier than the desk itself: a bobble-headed hula doll that looked like it had melted a bit in the heat.

What he pulled out of the desk did intrigue Paige a bit, although she didn't show it.

She didn't know that Mr. Pearson noticed her straightening up in her seat, raising her eyes from the ugliest bobble-headed hula doll he'd ever run across.

"I've got this idea, Paige," he said, shoving the

if with an innocent heart. He didn't understand how

drawer closed and tapping a brand new, spiral bound, My Little Pony, 5-subject notebook in the center of his desk. "I got this as a gift for my niece, but wouldn't you know it, her mother got her one the day before. Now a girl can only have so much of these rainbow colored ponies, right?"

Paige wouldn't know. She'd never had one of those rainbow colored ponies before, not even on a pencil, but she sure wanted one.

So she nodded.

"I think you should save me a trip back to the store, because I bought it in my sister's town, and that's quite a distance to drive just to return a notebook. You can use it to write, draw, whatever"

Paige nodded again. But...

"What should I write about?"

"Whatever you want," Mr. Pearson told her, sitting back in his chair, hands still holding the notebook. "You could write about your friends, or about the new baby brother or sister you're about to get."

Paige scowled.

"You could write down all the best memories you have about your grandmother who just passed," he suggested softly. "It might help."

That of course made her fight back tears, and Mr. Pearson finally handed over the notebook, and excused Paige from the rest of the day of school.

<!-- * * * -->

sleep came to her so easily, after all she was accused

So Paige went straight home, got out the pencil her grandmother had given her at the start of the year, sharpened it with the sharpener that her father had attached to the phone table in the hallway, and started to draw.

She drew her family at Easter, her grandmother sitting next to her in church, praying with her eyes closed so you couldn't tell if she was alive or dead.

She drew her father, happy, with a tree in the back yard covered with money. Did she think money grew on trees? No, she knew it did not. But it was very nice to think about.

She drew her mother sitting in her favorite chair, smiling happily with a new baby in her lap. Paige was careful to draw the baby exactly how she wanted it, with dark hair and dark eyes, just like her grandmother had. It had to be a little girl, too, so she drew a bow in the baby's hair.

And finally, Paige drew herself. She drew herself with all the friends Bettie Sue said she couldn't have, and each one had a bunny or a chick by their side.

Paige held the biggest, fattest one of all.

She went to bed that night with the notebook and the previously forgotten pencil safely in its box hidden under her pillow.

<!-- * * * -->

The next day Paige woke up and got ready for school just like she had the day before. She carefully

of. It was the blessing of those who had slipped from

packed her notebook and pencil in her backpack. Since she couldn't have any friends, she would use them during recess. There was a table that the other kids who didn't have any friends sat at to read books and avoid the rejection of trying to join a group game. She could sit there and forget everything.

Paige got downstairs, and her mother and father were sitting together at the kitchen table. That was unusual—usually her mother was found bustling around the kitchen table, serving her father, tidying up the place. Even after her daddy lost his job, they never sat together. It was like, against the rules or something.

So Paige stood on the bottom step, watching them.

Her father noticed her first, and even though her grandmother had died just two days before and Paige still could feel the tears choking her throat, he was smiling.

"Paige, honey, come here," he said, catching her wrist as she came close, pulling her up on his lap.

"We have some...well, it's good news," her mother continued for him, also smiling. "Your grandma, bless her heart, she had a will. Do you know what a will is?"

Paige shook her head.

"It's a piece of paper, or several pieces of paper, that someone writes out before they die saying what the people who are still living should do with their things."

Paige nodded. Made sense. Maybe she should draw a will out, just in case she died soon.

reality into the depths of their own minds. A blessing,

"Well," her father continued, "your grandmother's will was pretty much like we expected. She left what she had to your mother, which wasn't much. Some jewelry and clothes. She gave us her house a long time ago. But your grandfather..."

Paige hadn't known him.

"He had a piece of paper attached to the end of her will. It wasn't legal or anything, just hidden."

"What did it say?"

Her father pulled a dirty wooden box that had been sitting in the center of the table, and set it in front of Paige.

"It told us how to find this."

Paige opened the box.

Inside was money.

A lot of money.

"It was buried out back, underneath that old tree you used to swing from," her mother said, tears of joy in her eyes. "It's enough to let your daddy start his own business. He won't have to find a job now, just make his own. He'll have people working for him!"

Paige was happy for her parents, although she couldn't be quite as happy as they seemed to be. After all, she'd still lost her grandmother.

She was sent off to school, and Paige's mind was spinning. Her daddy had found money by the tree, and she'd drawn a picture of a tree. A money tree. Money didn't grow *on* the tree, just under it.

It was a lot for an eight-year-old girl to take in.

School brought her back to reality. Bettie Sue was

and probably a curse.

being mean, as usual. Paige's friends were all sort of ignoring her, which hurt, but not as much as losing her grandmother. When lunch was over and recess began, she went out to the yard with her backpack, and got ready to draw some more.

But first, someone tapped on her shoulder.

It was her old best friend. Penelope. Behind her stood a very large group of girls, including Bettie Sue.

They all looked anxious, and Paige could only scowl.

"What do you want?"

"Um, Paige? We heard about your grandma, and we're really sorry. And your daddy, too. I'm sure he'll find a job soon."

Paige's scowl lessened. "Well, he's going to start his own business, so he'll be okay. Thanks."

Penelope looked genuinely happy for her friend.

"Well, we still want to give you something. Bettie Sue was real mean yesterday. Just because you didn't get all the stuff we got for Easter doesn't mean you can't play with us. But here."

Paige's eyes grew wide, so wide she was pretty surprised they didn't jump right out of her head.

Penelope was holding a giant, white, stuffed animal rabbit.

For Paige.

She reached out to touch it, and it felt just as soft as it looked.

"It feels just like my Ruby," Penelope informed her. "Softer than anything. I know it's not real, but I wanted

¶ He didn't blame her for what she had done,

you to have it, anyway."

Paige thought about her new notebook, and the pencil her grandmother had given her. About the drawings she'd made the day before. About her grandmother, who had been right.

It wasn't just a regular pencil after all.

though. Her actions were justified, from what he could

tell. Twenty-seven months before Mathilda Jones had

$\mathcal{Q}$ is for ...quickening

She felt it. It was a feeling in the air, surrounding her and filling all of her senses.

Suffocating her.

Quin stood from her desk and walked silently to the window. Opening the shutters, she looked down from her tower to the courtyard below.

There were no birds singing from the trees. The flowers, as if sensing the oncoming darkness, had pulled their petals close for safety.

It was past time for Quin to prepare. She thought she would have more of it, but this was not in her control.

"My lady," a servant said from just outside her doorway, panting, "something's wrong. The guards,

arrived in her cell, she had gone about making her

they've all disappeared. I can't find a single one of them!"

Quin didn't turn. She knew they would be gone. They would have fought, defended themselves. That's not how this battle was meant to go.

It came so much more quickly than she had expected.

"Go back downstairs, and take yourself and anyone who will go with you to the fruit cellar. There will be food there, and water. Do not arm yourself," she added as the woman started to move from the doorway.

"My lady?"

Now Quin turned from the window.

She looked at her bed, where her cat had been resting.

Nearly all the animals would be gone now.

She mourned his loss silently.

"No weapons. Not even a needle and thread. Go now, and no matter what happens, do not resist."

Would the servant listen to her? Perhaps, but some of the men who worked in her home would not. More people would be lost, and for so pointless a reason.

Pulling a cloak around her shoulders, no one left to do it for her now, Quin left her chambers.

<!-- * * * -->

The servant had been out of breath for good reason. Her mistress occupied the only room in the highest tower. It was built taller than any other, and

personal world a little bit safer by shoving her abusive

settled on the precise point of the hilltop. The towers that compromised the home Quin was now mistress of had been built by her grandmother who had been a bit of a sage, if you care to listen to such things.

She had seen this coming. When her grand-daughter was born, she gave up her bedchamber for the girl, and insisted that she be the only human allowed inside the room.

That would slow it down, she said.

No one had ever known what she had meant about that.

Her grandmother had left books for Quin, and as soon as she learned to read, she started deciphering the tomes that were written in no known language. There were clues, of course, but no one knew where to find them but Quin.

Now she might be the only one left. The only one who could stop this.

The Quickening.

<!-- * * * -->

There were always three choices, but Quin saw the people around her only ever acknowledge two.

Fight, or flight.

You stood your ground, you resisted; or, you ran away.

Why did no one choose the third option?

The path of least resistance.

Stay and do nothing.

husband down the stairs when he had been quite deep

When you did nothing, there was no friction, no point to grab on to, no way to spread.

That was Quin's choice, and as she walked down the stairs to the main floors, she prepared for it. She passed the faces of her family, preserved forever in oil and pigment on cloth canvas and displayed in ornate frames. They had always resisted, even her grandmother had when it was her time.

Fight for the land.

Fight for your will.

And the fact that Quin accepted everything that came her way and let it wash over her like a spring rain drove all of them mad.

They were happy to leave her to her tower.

Quin saw a child huddled in a corner, and she waved a hand in the girl's direction.

She fell asleep.

The best defense for the young.

Quin kept moving.

The banisters, carved with ornate decoration, worn smooth by thousands of hands running over their surfaces, steadied her on her way to the first balcony.

The musical instruments that were nearly constantly in use by the artists who lived in the castle were abandoned in the gallery by their performers.

Good, Quin sighed. Hopefully they picked up nothing else along their way to safety.

She had only had five years to train the household after her father passed. Her mother, crippled with grief, let her.

in his cups. But her grief—or perhaps just years of

Quin knew her mother would survive. She had used all her fight trying to save her husband.

And while Quin had tried to teach by example the ways that would help her household make it through this event, many merely called her mad.

She paid them handsomely, they did their jobs, and in the taverns in the village and countryside, made fun of the Crazy Queen.

She would cry for them later. For now, she had arrived.

Quin passed through the open towering hall doors, and came face to face with her grandmother's greatest fear.

It was there.

It was waiting.

<!-- * * * -->

Later it would be said that their Queen savaged the beast with a broadsword made of the purest crystal, for that was the only thing that could destroy such evil.

Even later, it was told that she used her magic to lock the destroyer in another plane of existence, trapped for a thousand years.

Only Quin knew the truth, and no one would have believed her, even after a thousand years had passed.

She had waited.

It passed through her.

Baptizing her.

And because there was nothing to hold on to after

abuse—caused her to go a little insane. She followed

it had found its target, it was lost.

The Quickening died as rapidly as it had come on.

up the death of her husband with the violent, heartless

stabbing of his mother and sister, leaving only her

young niece alive in the house she shared with them.

R is for...rucksack

*T*he bag was red canvas and was covered with pockets and buckles. The moment Rose saw it, she knew she had to have it.

"How much?"

The man holding court at this particular garage sale looked up from his magazine and set aside his beer. He peered at Rose, squinting in the sun.

"Not for sale," he grunted, and went back to his copy of *Reel Time*.

Rose blinked. Huhwhat?

"But you're having a sale. Why put it out if its not for sale?"

"It's not mine. Someone must have left it."

She looked down at the bag in her hand and hefted it a bit.

¶ Joseph Jones was known to be a violent, abusive

"But it feels empty."

The man shrugged.

Rose went ahead and opened the bag, and had her suspicions confirmed.

Nothing.

If it was empty, it wasn't likely left by someone who wanted it, right? And if it really wasn't his, someone had obviously left it in an effort to get rid of it. And Rose was completely willing to help in that particular endeavor if she could.

Yes, she was making some pretty big inferences based on weak evidence.

But she really, really wanted the bag.

"Listen, I'll give you ten dollars and my phone number. If someone comes looking for it, give them my number and I'll give it back to them, okay?"

The Garage Sale Guardian peered back up at Rose.

"Ten dollars for something that ain't mine?"

Rose nodded, and held out the bill.

He snapped it from her fingers, and after Rose dug around in her pockets a bit, she scribbled her phone number on the top half of her Taco Bell receipt from earlier that day and held that out as well.

He didn't even look at her that time, just grabbed the number, shoved it into his pocket, and flipped another page in his magazine.

She left before he could change his mind.

Rose loved a good yard sale.

She slung the bag on her back, and only felt a little silly walking around with an empty backpack.

man. It was entirely possible, though not wildly

She thought about stuffing her purse in it, because compared to her awesome new garage sale find her purse was positively gaudy.

Then thought became action. She was passing another garage sale. Dropping to one knee, she unzipped her purse, flipped the top of the bag open, and promptly dumped the contents inside.

"Hey, would you mind doing me a favor," she called out to the woman manning the money.

The woman smiled.

"Can I add this to your sale? You can keep whatever you sell it for. I just don't want it anymore."

She looked confused, but someone else was trying to get her attention, so the lady just waved Rose on.

Satisfied that it had found a good home, she dropped it on the ground next to a bunch of toy cars.

Adjusting the straps, Rose was off.

It settled well on her back, and soon she even forgot it was there. Rose walked out of the residential area of town, and into the moderately busy town center. She had actually left home with a purpose, to grab some stuff from the store, and search the library for any new releases.

The garage sales had just sidetracked her.

She was going to have to stop by the ATM for more cash, too. She'd spent her grocery money on the bag, and while she didn't regret the impulse, she did kind of regret that instead of eating something tasty for supper she'd be eating noodles for a week.

And no coffee.

believed, that he had learned his behavior at the hands

Damn it. She was going to miss her coffee.

She almost walked right by the money machine while thinking about her coffee, but when realizing she'd just gone three paces past, Rose did an about face and pulled the bag off her shoulders.

Wallet, wallet...where was her wallet?

That was the one bad thing about a spacious bag, she mused to herself as she dug around. No matter how few things you carried, they still managed to hide themselves in the space available.

Eventually, she resorted to moving aside and hunching down on the ground. She started pulling out lipstick, business cards, a book, her keys, change purse, pill box...everything was out of her purse.

No wallet.

"Shit."

How had that not managed to get dumped into her new bag? Her face was flush and her heart was racing. Someone was going to find her purse at that woman's sale, and "steal" her wallet.

She hastily shoved everything she'd removed and set on the grass back in her bag, double checking to make sure nothing was left behind this time, and set out at a very quick pace back the way she'd come.

Crap. How could she be so forgetful? Leaving her wallet in her purse, it was stupid!

She called herself names all the way back to the yard in question.

There was her old purse, and she felt a rush of relief when she saw it there.

of his mother. Since his father passed when Joseph was

"Hi again! Change your mind?"

Rose shook her head, but snatched up the purse anyway, digging inside.

It was empty.

"Damn it!"

"Are you okay?"

Rose cursed again. "No, not really," she said.

She just wanted to cry.

"What happened?"

Rose turned to look back in the direction of her apartment. "I lost my wallet," she said, her voice breaking. "I spent my last ten dollars on this bag, and then I hated my purse so I dumped all my stuff in the new bag, and I thought I left my wallet in my old purse, but it's not there."

"Are you sure you didn't just overlook it?" The woman reached back down for Rose's discarded shoulder bag and started opening pockets and putting her hands in. "Double check your other bag. Nobody has picked this up since you were here, so it's probably in there."

She didn't believe it; the woman was just trying to make her feel better, but she did it anyway. She sat down in the grass, not caring about the grass stains she was gaining on the back pockets of her favorite jeans, and pulled things out one at a time from her red canvas rucksack.

The last thing that came out was her wallet.

"I don't believe it," she whispered.

The woman smiled. "See? There you go! Do you

only five, and his elder sister only ten, it made sense to

want to take this with you just in case?"

Rose nodded. "I'd better. I'm sorry, I'm being so stupid today." She opened her wallet and looked through it. Everything appeared to be there.

"No problem," she said, walking off to help someone.

Rose didn't move. Something inside her new backpack caught her eye.

It was green, and rather thick around the middle.

Reaching in, she put her fingers around a rather thick wad of cash with a rubber band tied around the middle.

That had definitely not been there before.

And there was no way the other woman had slipped it in.

Looking around, Rose quickly stuffed the rest of her items back in her bag, including the icky old purse.

Before she left, she pulled a few bills off the top of the pile, and shoved them in her pocket.

And when she was several blocks away, and she had caught her breath, and her mind stopped racing, she pulled the bills from her pocket.

Twenties. Five of them from the pile.

She held them up to the light.

Real.

She wasn't going to need that ATM after all.

Bernard that Joseph would have picked up his habits

"Rose, what is it with you and that damn bag? It's ugly, and rumpled, and doesn't go at all with your dress."

Smiling at her friend, Rose simply reached in and pulled out some clear nail polish.

"And it has to weigh a damn ton! You've always got everything in there. I bet if I asked you for the kitchen sink, you could pull it out!"

Rose didn't respond to the ridiculous statement her friend had made, simply leaned down and held her friend's leg still as she fixed the start of the run in her stocking.

Her friend was right, of course. If the nail polish didn't fix the run, she would reach in and find a replacement stocking. If she ran out of money, she could pull out some more.

If she got mugged, she could pull out a gun.

That happened to her, once.

It was lucky, and once Rose had sorted out that things just sort of came and went from the bag, but it always had what she needed, she stopped worrying about the things that went missing.

But she never told anyone.

It was a secret she shared with her bag.

Rumpled.

Red.

Rucksack.

from the family members he spent the most time

around.

S is for...separation

"Hi, honey!"

"Ugh."

"Rough day?"

Simon returned the dog's snarl (the animal had never liked him) and dropped his briefcase on a dining table chair. "You could say that." He walked through to the kitchen, and gave his wife a kiss on the cheek before moving to the refrigerator to grab a beer. "How was it holding down the fort?"

"Oh, you know. I pretended to organize, actually dusted and vacuumed, dirtied some dishes, am washing them now, but mostly I just stared at the television and let my brain rot."

"Sounds nice."

Serena shrugged. "It was. Except for the vacuuming

¶ It could be argued that Mathilda had saved Jane

part, when I broke the vacuumer."

"The vacuum cleaner is broken?"

"I think so," she replied as Simon walked out of the room. She hadn't meant to break it, of course. She'd taken a look at it, and the little whirring thing that usually spun frantically picking up all the dirt and dust wouldn't go around in circles any more. It was snagged in place by an amazingly large amount of long brown hair.

Her hair was brown, so technically it was her fault. The only thing that concerned her was how she had managed to lose so much without realizing it!

Which of course had sent her to the bathroom in a frenzy. How much hair could a girl lose before she needed to be on the women's version of Rogaine?

She hadn't actually watched any television at all. Once she started inspecting her hairline, she had found gray hairs. At thirty! And like any sane person, she started to pluck them out, one by one. And then she realized that she had a giant pile of gray hairs in her bathroom sink, which sent her into a panic and she washed them down before she realized that it would cause the sink to stop up, and...

"Damn it, honey, did something happen to the sink?"

Serena cringed.

"Um, sorry! Just a little accident with the vacuum!" In a round about sort of way.

Simon didn't answer.

She hadn't expected him to.

the fate she herself had suffered. Bernard chose to

He was very, very good at putting up with her serious lack of homemaker skills. He put up with all sorts of things from her, actually, and she loved him for it.

He loved her, too. They'd just gotten married a few months before, and he brought her flowers every Friday, like clockwork. He'd never done it while they were dating—he said he wanted to establish romantic, married habits.

Some things he did Serena didn't like as much. Simon worked an awful lot, and didn't want her to work at all. She was bored stupid in the house all day, but she kept things clean, and went for walks sometimes by the park, and got to stare jealously at all the women with the baby bassinets and playing with their kids.

She'd also started a blog. It was something she was ninety percent sure that Simon would hate, but she had a lot to say, and already had a pretty big following. She thought maybe after a while she would be popular enough to get advertisers on her site, and that the extra money would make Simon happy, and then he could work less.

It was just a thought, anyway.

"Oh! Simon," she called out towards the living room as she finished drying her hands and putting the dish towel on the oven handle like he liked it, "you got some mail today!"

Simon always liked to see the mail soon after he got home, but before dinner. Grabbing the pile, she took it into the living room and dropped it on his lap.

believe the best of the woman, though she was quite

Plopping herself onto the sofa on his left, she looked at him eagerly.

"Well, aren't you going to open it? I weeded out all the junk. I'm just dying to see what's in that big manila envelope!"

So he picked that one up first. "I wonder what this is?"

"I know," she said, practically bouncing on the couch. "There's no return address. For a minute I thought maybe it was just junk, but then I thought, maybe it's one of those mystery envelopes you get when your spouse is cheating and some vindictive person has taken a bunch of photos and is ready to blackmail you!"

Serena loved a good mystery!

Simon swore.

She saw his hands were shaking.

He ripped open the envelope, and in his haste, ripped too far.

The contents spilled on the floor.

Jelly side up.

Serena swore, too.

"I want a divorce."

out of her mind now. But then, he had a lot of time

to watch over and observe her. It was easy to hear her

heartbreaking cries of pain for Joseph to stop whatever

T is for...target

I t was the twentieth day of the month, and a Tuesday. Talya watched her arm with trepidation from the very second the day started right until the moment when the mark appeared.

When it did, she could no longer stand to look at the appendage.

She was tainted.

Talya got dressed shortly after, switching her usual sleep garb of tank top and boxers for long sleeves that reached her fingertips and a long, heavy skirt. Her boots reached her knees, and she pulled a hood up on her head.

Anyone who saw her would know her shame. She could at least avoid seeing it on their faces.

pain he was inflicting on her in her memories, and to

The streets were busy that day, full of pedestrian workers making their way to their jobs, ready to slave away another day. Didn't they care that ten of their fellow workers had just lost their livelihood? Didn't they care that ten of their brothers, sisters, children, and parents had just been targeted?

Didn't they notice?

Talya knew the answer. They knew, but chose to ignore.

Every time she hadn't been chosen she rejoiced quietly, but rejoiced just the same that it had not been her arm that had been marked.

When coworkers showed up dressed in clothing too warm for the season, and then didn't come back after their noon break, she quietly gave thanks that it wasn't her.

She wouldn't say goodbye to her friends. They wouldn't want the reminder that someone so close to them had been chosen. In fact...

Why was she even bothering going to work? Surely the system that managed to mark their citizens with a genetically engineered tattoo would be able to locate her when the time came, even if she wasn't in her assigned place.

Talya was going to do the impossible. The ridiculous. The insane.

She did not get on her assigned train that morning. When the locomotive pulled into her station and the doors opened in front of her, she let the tide of people slip around her while her feet stayed anchored to the

have sympathy for her.

platform.

The doors closed in front of her.

Nobody looked in her direction.

The train pulled out, leaving her and no one else on the platform.

Talya started walking.

<!-- * * * -->

"How is the collection going?"

A young man in a blue lab coat snapped to attention. "Very good, sir. Nine of ten have been retrieved and are in stasis."

"And the tenth?"

Tad didn't want to say anything. He knew the report he had wasn't the one his supervisor wanted to hear.

"The tenth didn't appear at her position today."

"Residence?"

"Not there, either. It doesn't appear that she ran—her things are still there, as if she just walked out the door and disappeared."

Tad found himself on the receiving end of a deadly expression.

"Well, has her tag been activated?"

"She doesn't have one, sir."

Tad braced himself for the inevitable explosion that followed.

"Why doesn't she have a tag?" his supervisor asked slowly, as if trying to get information from a child.

"I don't know, sir. I'm working on that now."

¶ Leaving the window and letting the murderer

"I want a report in thirty minutes, and if you don't have that last sample in your possession in that time, you can take her place!"

Tad spun in his chair and began working furiously with the controls in front of him. He knew the threat was mostly an empty one. His position on the station was one he'd been bred for, and another one wouldn't be manufactured for another three years, and would need two years of training on top of that.

But his supervisor's anger was real.

Tad went to work finding the missing sample.

Talya found herself walking along the train tracks. She had started walking thinking that she would be leaving the train station and going back home until they collected her, but there had been a flaw in her plan.

The entrances she'd used had been sealed. The exits were on the other side of the station, and so Talya had lowered herself to the rails thinking she would just climb up the other side and leave.

But then she'd discovered a service walkway, and curiosity won.

Talya started walking in the direction the train arrived from every morning.

Maybe she'd reach another town—there were always a few people on the train when it reached her station.

sleep, Bernard opened the letter that Mathilda had

Maybe she'd find the trains originating terminal.

But she didn't find either of these.

Talya walked for a long time. She hadn't had breakfast, and her stomach made rumbling noises.

Occasionally she saw something move in the corner of her eye, but when she turned her head to get a look she saw nothing but small birds.

There was no one to look at her down here in the tunnel, and even though the temperature stayed the same, cool, she quickly grew too warm for her longs sleeves and hood. Removing them, tying her sweater around her waist, her arm was now quite visible.

In the pool of light provided by a service lantern, Talya stopped to study it.

The tattoo was extensive, wrapping from her palm to her elbow. The design was like nothing she'd seen before, not even on other selectees.

Of course, she'd not often seen the tattoo of another selectee. Without fail they covered their arms after being selected, and it was only when they pushed a sleeve up without thinking that she'd caught a glimpse.

Hers was full of straight lines and the occasional circle. It was several shades darker than her skin, but not quite black. Almost like her skin had been burned and the char had flaked off, leaving only dead skin in its place.

But her arm still felt like it always did. Poking it in the dark spots, she felt no difference than in the light.

When Talya looked up this time, she didn't see a flash of movement.

written. After a quick glance it was obvious that it was

She saw someone standing ten paces ahead, standing very, very still.

They were smiling.

Welcoming.

"Hello," the person said.

Talya wanted to run.

"Don't run. I'm not here to collect you." The person held up their own arm, their hand palm out to her, letting their long sleeve fall down to reveal another selection tattoo.

Talya was frightened and relieved at the same time. Her hand nervously covered her arm as much as she could.

"Do you want to join us?"

"Us?"

The other person nodded. "Don't worry. They won't find you down here."

Despite her nerves, Talya finally nodded, and followed the stranger into the dark.

Into safety.

<!-- * * * -->

Tad found the missing sample just before his deadline ended.

"She self-terminated," he reported to his supervisor. "Just jumped into the tracks. The next train arrived on schedule, and she would have been crushed."

His supervisor gave a heavy sigh. "Why do the selectees from this region keep doing that?"

the same letter she had written 26 times previously,

Tad shook his head, relieved that he was now safe from his supervisor's wrath. "I don't know, sir. Perhaps we ought to start retrieving the selectees earlier?"

The older man sighed. "No. If they're predisposed to self-termination we would just lose them in stasis. Losing them down there is less paperwork and clean up for us."

Tad nodded.

"Well, then. Get ready for the next selection. We've only got twenty days to prepare. It's going to come faster than we think."

"It always does, sir."

Tad turned back to his work.

Another one had escaped.

He wondered whether his replacement in five years would keep up the ruse? He wondered if the next supervisor, due to come on duty in seven years would believe it if he did.

It probably wouldn't matter. By that time, their numbers would be stronger, and they would have started their own families. They would have a reason to resist.

Maybe the Targeting could finally stop.

with little change. Every month she appeared to wake

from the screaming, cursing haze where her heart was

U is for…unavailable

*D*ude. What's wrong with your roommate?"

Una looked at Ursula who was hunched over her laptop, as usual, typing frantically away at who knew what.

Seriously—you couldn't see. The girl kept a protection screen on like you usually only saw at the doctor's office so unless you were like two inches away, all you saw was black.

"I have no clue. She's been doing that ever since I moved in over Christmas break. I tried talking to her, but she just acts like she doesn't hear. But she keeps her side of the room clean, doesn't leave crumbs around to attract bugs, so I pretty much just do my thing and she just…"

alternately breaking, then burning with hate. She would

"Types?"

"Pretty much all day until around two in the morning." Una held up a black pair of serious headphones. "She left these on my bed one morning after I overslept for my class."

"Wow."

Una shrugged. "Whatever. Dan, are we going out, or what?"

"We're going," he said, his attention finally back on her.

Where it belonged, Una thought, satisfied.

Una returned several hours later after a complete date failure. Dan was a sleaze, which she had sort of known when she accepted the date, but she thought maybe he would pretend to be decent at least through dinner.

Unfortunately, that wasn't the case, which is why she was now sneaking through the dorm with a case of beer she'd rescued from a frat party.

She could hear the tapping from the hallway as she came out of the stairwell to her floor. It was Ursula's familiar rhythm, a sound that Una was now sure she could separate from hundreds of others.

Huh. Maybe she could submit that to a game show or something. "Name That Tap".

"Hi, Ursula," she greeted as she closed the door behind her. It was kind of like living with a doll—Una

sit down at her secretary which she generally avoided

had tried just being quiet, but she felt just as strange trying to ignore her roommate as she found being ignored. So when she caught Ursula smiling once when she told a joke, she assumed the other girl was listening.

"I've got beer, if you want one. Still cold. I'm pretty sure the Alpha Gamma Nu Mu Schmoos won't miss it."

Without asking, Una reached around and set a beer on Ursula's coaster. She took her own, opened it, and plopped down on her bed.

"Dan was a complete jerk. He was trying to put his hands where they didn't belong before we even got seated at the restaurant. I didn't even get food! So I snagged a case of beer from one of the alphabet parties. I probably ought to order pizza or something. You want pizza?"

Una didn't wait for an answer. She wasn't going to get one. Instead she reached for her phone, called the local pizza joint, and ordered enough for both of them.

Everyone liked cheese, right?

"I hate it when men act like they own you, you know? I probably would have slept with him if he'd got me drunk enough. But he couldn't even wait that long. Honestly."

Una sighed, wondering what to do until the pizza arrived. For a while she watched Ursula type, and wondered how the woman never seemed to get out of the chair, or pee, or do anything but type, and not weigh like three hundred pounds. She judged her roommate

as if it didn't exist, take the one sheet of paper that was

weighed something more like ninety pounds, soaking wet. Her feet barely touched the floor.

She spent about five minutes on her tablet before she got bored of that, too.

"Ursula, what do you know about guys? I mean, I thought I was pretty good with them, but I keep picking up losers here. They're all boneheads with their heads in the gutter. I probably ought to start picking guys who study well instead of just look good, but I can't help myself!"

Una's tirade was interrupted by a knock on their door.

"Who's that? There's no way the pizza got here this quickly."

But that's exactly who was there.

"Pizza for Ursula?"

Una looked back at her roommate, who of course was not looking up from her computer. "Um, I'll pay. What kind of pizza is it?"

"Pepperoni and green olive."

"Let me grab my wallet."

<!-- * * * -->

Una fell asleep, or fell unconscious, about ten minutes after her last beer. Ursula waited until she was out cold, then finally stopped her typing. She cleaned up the pizza, glad that her friend had enjoyed it. Canceling the cheese pizza that Una had ordered had been a risk, but that woman was stuck in a rut with more than just

there along with the one quill, and use it to slice open

her love life. It wasn't a type she'd ever seen her try before, and she liked the idea of introducing Una to new experiences.

Like men. Ugh, the losers she brought back. It was insane how she could continue to pick such losers. The odds were even in her favor—at some point she was bound to end up with someone decent.

Still, though, the girl obviously needed some help.

Ursula put the rest of the beer cans in the refrigerator, then rinsed and crushed the cans so the R.A. wouldn't find them. The trash went into a bag that she set by the door.

She doubted that Una would hear her typing tonight.

Ursula used her roommate's phone to send a text to the boy she'd been studying with lately. Brian was the kind of guy Una needed. Solid, steady, good looking, but quiet. Respectful.

Ursula would date him herself if she wasn't already unavailable.

After sending the text, an innocent, slightly drunk sounding something that ought to cause the desired outcome in the morning, Ursula went back to her computer.

She began to type.

her fingertips. Blood would become the ink with which

she wrote her letters to her deceased husband, the man

$\mathcal{V}$ is for...vacant

$\mathcal{I}$t was perfect.

"So, how much is it?"

The question was superfluous. She was going to take it anyway. But people liked to hear you asking the right questions when they were suspicious about your motive.

It made them feel better.

"Four hundred thousand," the agent said. "It's the entire building plus the parking across the street. Zoned commercial."

"And you said it was last used simply as a warehouse?"

"Yes, but it's been empty for about five years. There's a lot of work to do to get things cleaned up, and there will probably be quite a few squatters and such hiding

she loved even as she hated and feared him.

in the corners. I know a company..."

"I'll take it." Violet didn't want to hear about his company. She could take care of her own messes.

The real estate agent didn't think so, obviously. She was dressed far too uptown for this location. Her skirt was tight and short, her blazer open and her blouse showing that she wasn't taking the cold weather too seriously with the amount of skin she was showing. She had to watch where she walked so her heels didn't fall through a crack and send her flying.

"Well, we can go work up the paperwork back in my office then," the agent replied with a smile.

He was glad to be out of there. He wasn't comfortable, with Violet or the location. She could tell; his fear was tangible.

"Yes, let's finish this off. Do you think they'd agree to immediate possession? I don't want to wait for settlement to get to work."

<!-- * * * -->

Money talked, and the entire amount paid in cash to the seller did indeed let her have access to the property before they cleared escrow. She didn't bring in a team, she took care of everything herself.

First she drained the building of life. Starting with the first floor and working up, giving her prey time to panic and gather all in one spot. It made the job so much easier. There were one or two cats she considered turning, thinking they could be quite attractive if they

¶   She used another pool of blood as if it were wax,

cleaned up, but she couldn't bring herself to hurt the poor creatures.

She allowed them to leave.

The human inhabitants weren't so lucky.

A few drug addled teenagers, several elderly homeless, and one prostitute hiding from her pimp, all bitten, drained, and turned to dust. So simple, no bodies to hide, just a little sweeping, at some point.

She could hire that done.

And when her building was clear, she started on the real work.

Hiring an appropriate contractor to whip the place into decent shape.

<!-- * * * -->

Violet was nearing on five hundred years. She had turned on her thirty-fourth birthday, and she hadn't been happy about it at first, because who liked to be savagely bitten on the neck and then forced to go through a completely agonizing process to become immortal? Especially on the eve of the anniversary of ones thirty-fifth birthday, where one was about to spend another entire year as a virginal example of purity.

It was crap.

Why couldn't it have happened on the eve of her twenty-fifth birthday?

But one worked with what one had, and she'd made the best of it, for quite a few years. Now she was ready to start over. Build a new life.

pressing his ring into it to "seal" the letter. Then she

Sleep for a while.

Just a while.

And an old building, acting like it was older than she, for goodness sake, with the holes in the floor and rotting wood, it was as good a disguise as any. She'd gotten it cheap—after five hundred years, you could save up quite a little nest egg, and the building purchase made hardly a dent. She could spent twice that getting it all fixed. Turn it into a lovely resting place.

Violet didn't know why she was so tired. There really was no earthly reason. She had been awake nearly ever moment since she'd been bitten and turned into this blood-sucking immortal. And now...she didn't look it, but she felt it. The undeniable urge to close her eyes, just for a moment. Except she had a feeling that moment would last a bit longer than a moment. Or even a few hours of moments.

When Violet fell asleep, she was going to be there for quite some time.

Which was dangerous.

And why she was taking a ten story warehouse and turning it into a long-term bedroom.

You know, just in case she was there for longer than a year or so.

She walked through the finished building, her impossibly tall heels clicking on the marble floors in the foyer. Vince the security guard, one of her own, nodded her way. The crush of people waiting for elevators parted for her as she walked purposefully towards her private lift.

would throw the ring into the fire, and it would be up

It was an odd effect she had on these humans. They knew she was there, but purposely avoided her. Almost like she gave off an aura of "leave me alone or I'll hurt you". Or like a reverse magnetic field. She was wired differently, and they bounced away from her.

Violet had been bothered at first. Now it was almost useful.

Her elevator looked just like the others, but nobody used hers but her.

The avoidance thing again.

She entered it, and hit the button for the 8th floor.

Perhaps it had been an odd choice, but she hadn't wanted to be on the top floor. What would happen if the building somehow began to fall apart? She didn't want to be the first one to be vulnerable when that time came. She wanted some time for Vince to get her out.

Or, you know, whomever was still around to care.

So she'd taken the top floor of her building and turned it into a hotel of sorts. Where people like her could rest in safety. Not as much safety as her, of course. Her suite was on the 8th floor, with two floors above and two below of suites for hemoglobin-deficient creatures. Her bedroom was in the center of the floor, reinforced, with security inside and out. Nobody entered the 8th floor but her. They all knew she was there, but it was her building, so she could sleep wherever she wanted.

The rest of the building was leased out to humans. They would help keep the money flowing while she slept, and Vince and a few others she'd gotten to know over the years would manage things until she was

to Bernard to retrieve it before the next fire was built so

feeling better. When she woke, they could take their turns.

Just not in her bed.

The elevator doors opened on her floor. The decor was impeccable, a minimalist theme she was sure would never go out of style. Or at the very least, come back into fashion in a couple decades if it came to that. She passed the giant plants—plastic—and mourned the dust she would have to deal with when she woke.

Down a hallway, turn left, then right, another left. It was a maze and it was difficult to navigate, it was feng shui, and it was on purpose.

A girl couldn't be too careful.

Finally she reached her room. This one was not feng shui, it was chaotic. Everything she'd ever loved in her life was here, surrounding her. Her favorite colors, her favorite memories, things she'd collected. And in the center, an enormous bed.

She'd thought about a coffin. Something more traditional. But Violet was claustrophobic.

She wore nothing to bed. She climbed between the satin sheets and wondered briefly how long it would take for them to fall apart from age. Nobody was going to come in to change her linens.

Crap. She'd forgotten to set the alarms.

Back up, padding across the floor in bare feet, then back between the sheets. It felt amazing to finally relax. It hadn't felt this good to lay down in about four hundred and seventy-five years. Come to think about it, that was the last time she'd...

she could wear it again when she woke.

<!-- * * * -->

Vince turned his head as a new security feed came through his usual loop. He looked and saw Miss Violet in bed, fast asleep. It was good. He would look out for her, and then she could look out for him when his time came.

Nobody noticed he was the only security guard on duty. They actually didn't pay much attention to him at all. And taking care of troublemakers at night was easier for him than most men in his position.

Just a little dust to sweep up when he was done.

¶ Bernard folded the letter again, and placed the

letter with the other 26, in the glowing embers of his

W is for...wander

"**W**here ya going?"

Walt looked down at the dirty little boy trailing alongside her. "Nowhere, really."

"Mom says you're looking for something."

"Yeah? What's that supposed to be?"

"You. You're looking for you." The kid kicked a rock. "What's that mean?"

Walt shook her head. "Ask your mom."

"She'll just tell me to go play."

"Then go play."

The kid kept up for a bit, then obviously getting bored with the slow pace, ran off to join a couple of friends.

That suited Walt just fine.

own roaring fire. He sat back on the stool that was

Walt, actually Waltrina, had run away from home.

She'd left behind...well, she didn't like to think what she'd left behind. Suffice to say that at thirty years of age, she had not left behind two sobbing, distraught parents wondering what had happened to their little girl.

Some of the less disturbing things she'd left behind...well, she'd left behind her hair. Cut it clean off, combed some shoe polish through what was left, and slapped a cap on her head that she kept pulled down low over her eyes. It was enough to trick little kids, and nobody else really dared to get close enough to tell.

She'd also left behind her ladylike senses. She had left with the clothing on her back, but no money. She slept where she could find a protected spot, used the bathroom where nobody was looking, and avoided towns wherever she could.

Bathing? Yeah, she left that behind, too.

Since she was the only one who had to put up with the smell, nobody complained. Certainly not her. She had bigger things to worry about.

Like food. Did she mention she'd left behind money, as well?

Walt reached up to play with the hair that stuck out from under her hat. One foot in front of the other, repeat, repeat, repeat...

Her stomach growled.

Sighing, she realized she now had to do what she'd been dreading for the past two days.

Bathe.

his station. Watching the letter burn, he wondered if

If she took a dip in the river she'd been following, cleaned off herself and her clothes, she could probably find work of some sort that would get some food in her stomach.

She didn't want to talk to anyone.

She didn't want to eat, really.

But she didn't want to die.

It was bath time.

<!-- * * * -->

"Waltrina? Come on, Walt, come out here. I just want to talk to you."

"I don't want to talk," she mumbled from behind the door.

"We have to talk about this sometime. We can't ignore it forever."

"I can."

Her husband had gotten tired of trying to reason with her from behind the closed door, and finally left her alone. That was one of Walt's mutant abilities—she could out-wait just about anyone.

But she couldn't out-wait her situation. As soon as he'd left for work, she'd left the house.

<!-- * * * -->

And now here she was, shaking the memories out of her head, about to step into the water fully clothed. She wasn't looking forward to it. The weather

Mathilda's husband would receive the letter in hell.

hadn't warmed up enough for getting in the river to be refreshing, only freezing.

She was up to her knees and creeping in slowly before being startled into complete submersion.

"What do you think you're doing?"

Walt came up sputtering. She wiped the water from her eyes, and found shoe polish all over her hands. It was probably dripping down her face and neck and staining her clothing. With a sigh, she dunked her head again, this time on purpose.

"Get out of that water this instant," the voice commanded her as she came out of the water for a second time. "You'll catch your death from cold out here!"

Walt didn't disagree. While the water had been shockingly cold at first, now her head and shoulders, soaked through, froze in the cool spring air.

"Come on, come on, we have to hurry before the cold sets in."

Walt nodded, choosing her steps carefully on the slippery river bottom. She didn't look at who was speaking to her, just concentrated on getting out of the water.

When she made it out, a woman that couldn't be much older than Walt was staring at her disapprovingly.

She stood there, shivering. Waiting either for the woman to tell her what to do, or leave her alone.

"Get undressed. I have a blanket for you to wrap up in. You can't walk around in that wet stuff."

<!-- * * * -->

"I don't have any other clothes," Walt finally said, refusing to get undressed. She was vulnerable enough. What had she been thinking, trying to take a bath? It was almost like she *did* want to die, because what she'd just done surely had been a death wish.

"I did just say I have a blanket, did I not? Don't worry, I won't look."

It didn't really occur to Walt to disagree. She had spent her life planted firmly in the spheres of controlling women and men. When you did what they asked, life was pleasant.

Walt really didn't like life to be unpleasant.

So with the woman's back turned, Walt did her best to get undressed quickly. She left her underwear on. There was no way she was parting with those. Then if she needed to run, she wouldn't be completely nude.

The blanket brushed the ground as she pulled it tight around her neck and shoulders. There was no way to fasten it except with her fists, so she dropped the sopping clothing to the ground, and waited for the woman to turn again.

"Are you done yet?"

Walt's stomach let out a loud rumble in response.

The woman spun around and didn't wait for an answer. Seeing her discarded clothing on the ground, she scooped the pile up, and waved for Walt to follow. Wringing the excess water out, the stranger walked ahead of her.

"Really, what were you thinking? You're damned lucky I walked up on you. You obviously don't know

¶   In a small room some distance away from her only

the river, or you would have realized you were about three inches from a drop-off and an undercurrent strong enough to sweep you three miles downriver before you had a chance to pop your head back up above water. Now my truck is parked just over here. We'll go into town—I own a laundromat, and we can wash your clothes and get you something to eat. You'll wear some of my...some of Will's old clothes. They'll need to be cinched up, but at least you'll be warm until your stuff is done."

Walt got into the truck. It wasn't in her nature to disagree. Maybe this would be okay. Maybe it would work. She'd get some supper and then could work at the laundromat for a few days to earn some money before she moved on. Maybe she could even buy some of those old clothes the lady was going to put her in tonight.

She filtered out the ramblings of her rescuer, watched the landscape fly by outside her window much faster than it had been during her pedestrian wanderings, and concentrated on thinking forward, and not behind.

<!-- * * * -->

"I'm afraid you're sterile, Waltrina."
"What does that mean?"
"You'll never be able to have children."
"Never?"
The doctor had shaken his head no, apologized, and

living family, a young girl named Jane played with her

left Walt in his office so she could compose herself.

It was a lot to think about, and she could feel the knowledge pushing down on her, pushing all the air from her lungs. The only thing Walt had ever wanted was to be a mother, to raise her own child as she wished she had been raised.

No loud voices.

No hands raised in anger.

No restrictions on what was available to read, whether her child could have friends, or how she ought to think.

Her fiancé had arrived then. Late, he burst into the doctor's office.

"Where is he? What did he say? I'm so sorry I'm late, darling. Traffic was horrendous."

"I'll marry you," Waltrina breathed in a hoarse whisper, the weight of the doctor's words still weighing down her shoulders.

If she couldn't have children, it didn't matter if she married someone just like her parents. Someone who thought and acted just like them. Someone they approved of.

It wasn't worth fighting for what she wanted if she couldn't have children.

<!-- * * * -->

So much for thinking forward. Walt wiped a tear from her cheek as she pulled herself back into the present.

pet. She spent her days in quiet solitude, her only break

"Honey, are you okay? Are you hurt or something?"

Walt shook her head. "I'm fine, thanks." She took a bite from the enormous plate of food she had been served by Wendy, the woman who had fished her out of the river.

She wasn't going to think about him, or her situation right now. She was going to think about this moment. Her needs right now.

She needed to ask a favor.

"Do you know of anybody in town needing some part time help right now?"

Wendy looked thoughtful. "Maybe. How long are you staying?"

Walt shrugged. Long enough to earn about a month's worth of food money. "I don't really have a plan," she answered honestly.

"Well, where were you headed before I found you?"

Walt paused before answering. "West."

Wendy snorted as she picked up her plate and took it to the sink. "That's vague."

Walt ate another bite, then set down her fork. "I feel pretty vague. Thanks for the food, but I can't eat all this."

Wendy turned, hands still washing the small army of dishes she'd used to create the feast Walt couldn't bring herself to finish. "What? Don't you like it?"

"I just can't finish. Actually, I kind of need to use your bathroom."

coming when the lovely teacher came to visit for their

Walt didn't wait for directions. She had passed it earlier, and now she rushed to it as quickly as possible.

Bent over the toilet bowl, heaving up the food that had been so delicious only a moment before, Walt felt a cool cloth on the back of her neck. A gentle hand rubbed her back as she waited to see if anything else was going to come up.

"Are you okay now?"

Walt stared at the back of her eyelids for a moment, then nodded. She heard the toilet flush, and let Wendy help her up. She was led to a sofa, and Wendy joined her a moment later, handing her a glass of water.

Wendy waited until Walt had drank most of the glass, rinsing the taste of bile from her mouth, before asking, "Honey, how far along are you?"

<!-- * * * -->

Walt had taken her wedding and engagement rings and dropped them in the bowl where her husband left his keys every day after work. The sound they made was final, the ring of gold against crystal. He would find them there, and he would know she had left.

Her hand practically floated without the weight of those oppressive shackles. She had never wanted anything so fancy. But the people in her life were not accustomed to thinking about what Walt might want. They never even considered asking.

Her husband had left with the driver, so there was

daily talks. She had rows of dolls and stacks of books,

no one to ask if she wanted a ride. The housekeeper had today off, and the new housemaid was so concerned with not bothering the master that she kept to herself. She wouldn't dare ask the mistress where she was going.

Walt had let herself in to the chauffeur's rooms, and raided his closets. She made sure to take everything of hers along when she left the room—she didn't want to get him in trouble.

She didn't look back at the house as she left the alley behind it and walked out onto the busy street. Her shoes and socks were the only things now on her body that were hers.

It was dark, but she hadn't worried. She couldn't imagine living one more moment with a husband who insisted it was her wifely duty to make love to him when there was no love between them. She couldn't sit idle for one more day, pretending to enjoy the visits from the simpering women trying to impress her mother.

The darkness outside couldn't scare her more than the emptiness inside her could.

<!-- * * * -->

"I'm not pregnant," Walt finally said to Wendy. "I'm barren. I can't ever be pregnant."

She couldn't stop the silent tears that followed.

And she couldn't stop her story from pouring out, either. She told Wendy everything, from the moment she met her husband, to the doctor's visit, to when she

blocks that built towers and buildings, and plenty of

finally found the courage to leave.

When she was done, Wendy scooped her into a comforting hug, and Walt let the fear and sorrow and loneliness she'd felt over the past few weeks pour out in her sobs. When she finally cried the last tear she had, Wendy let her go.

"You were sick from not eating," Wendy told her. "You'll stay here until you've got your strength up. You can decide what to do when I know you aren't going to keel over."

Walt looked at the woman sitting next to her on the sofa. She didn't mind this woman telling her what to do. For the first time, it was for her own good, and they both knew it.

It was time for Walt to stop wandering.

pretty clothes. It was a lovely life, and there was never

anyone to yell at her, or interrupt her play. She could

X is for...xenolith

It hit just after two a.m. on the fifth day of December, the year 2032.

Right through her ceiling, slowed by the efforts of both her roof and her second floor, it crashed through her mattress, between her feet, and lodged itself somehow in the floorboards of the first floor.

Xenia, of course, woke up immediately.

Her bed was on fire—it was hard to sleep when your bed is on fire.

She quickly doused it with the glass of water she kept on the bedside stand. Then when she was sure it was out (after poking the charred bed with her toe and finding it warm and wet), she scrambled around and stuck her head through the hole.

Of course she couldn't see anything. The lights

do what she liked, and she liked being left to entertain

were out. Except she could see something, and it was kind of pinkish and glowing.

Still, she lunged out of bed, hit the switch, and fell to the floor to look under her bed this time.

A rock. A meteorite. Glowing pink, but, as she put her hand close to the rock, found that it wasn't hot, but rather quite cool to the touch.

"Weird."

"What is?"

"Dude, Xander, look at this thing," Xenia said, scooting over on the cold wooden floor.

Her roommate, housemate, whatever—the guy who helped pay the rent but didn't sleep in her bed—got on the floor next to her.

"Wow, what the hell?"

Xenia rolled over on her back, and saw through the bed the gaping hole in her ceiling, and then roof, showing the stars outside.

"It just sort of dropped in on me."

"Duh. You're lucky you didn't get hit with it, Xen."

She nodded. "Do you suppose they have insurance for stuff like this?"

Xander shrugged, now laying on his back as well.

The rock, about the size and shape of a football, was in his hands.

"I suppose you'll find out when you call the adjuster in a few hours."

"Let me see that," Xenia said, taking the rock from his hands. "Geez, this is light. What do you suppose it is?"

herself.

"I dunno. Black? Last I checked, I failed geography."

"Geology," Xenia corrected.

"Right. I'm going back to bed. It's not supposed to rain tomorrow, so you should be okay sleeping in here, right?"

"Don't worry," she said with a smile, pulling herself to her feet and then offering a hand to Xander, setting the meteorite on her bed. "I'm not going to launch myself into your bed just because a rock hit the house."

"See that you don't. 'Night, Xen."

"Goodnight."

Not that it wouldn't be worth her time to launch herself into his bed, if he were interested, Xenia pondered. He had a very nice butt. His pajama pants hung nicely on it.

But, looking up at the ceiling and the gaping hole that was slightly larger than the piece of mystery rock that had fallen through it, she couldn't sleep in her room any more tonight. With her luck, a bird would come in and mistake her face for his morning restroom break, and she didn't need that kind of good morning in...oh, look, she only had three more hours before her alarm would go off.

She grabbed her phone, left the rock on her bed, and went to sleep on the sofa in the living room.

Quietly, and with no more damage to her roof.

¶ But her teacher was to arrive soon, and looking

Xenia left the house at her regular time, wearing her regular outfit, with her regular bag, plus one. She maneuvered the additional pouch over her shoulder then set her backpack over her shoulders after it, more or less securing it in place. Climbing on her bicycle, she managed the ride to work with minimal effort.

She'd given up her car during her divorce, and while at first she simply couldn't afford any other mode of transportation than the bicycle she'd picked up at a garage sale for fifty dollars and fixed for another hundred, she'd grown to enjoy it quickly. She'd never been much of a runner, and she was pleased as punch to find the zen she'd often envied her running friends reaching during their exercise regimens. Plus, after a few sweaty months, she'd stopped perspiring like a couch potato running a marathon and enjoyed the exercise.

At the school, she even got a little extra in her paycheck for not using one of the precious on-campus parking spots that would have otherwise been assigned to her.

Green bonus!

Her lecture was early, and after delivering it to an auditorium full of obnoxious overachievers and hungover slackers, she locked her purse in her closet—uh, office—and made a beeline for The Rock Gods.

"Can I help you?"

She'd been wandering for a bit in the appropriate building, and finally someone had taken pity on her.

"Please. I need to talk to the person most likely to

forward to that visit now, she put her pet aside and sat

know what this is," Xenia said as she opened up her satchel to reveal its contents.

"Oh, that's interesting. Where'd you find that?"

"Under my bed," Xenia replied.

She was rewarded with a startled look.

"May I touch it?"

"Are you the person I need to talk to?"

"Dr. Zachary, at your service." He stuck a thumb under the staff badge he had pinned to the hem of his shirt.

"Xenia," she said, holding out her hand. "Nobody can ever pronounce my last name, so it's easier for me just not to tell you so you don't have to try."

He smiled, shook her hand, and glanced at her own name tag.

His eyes bulged.

Xenia held back a snicker.

"Well, then," he finally managed. "Just Xenia, would you like to see my lab?"

"I thought you'd never ask," she replied with a smile.

Dr. Zachary was kind of hot.

His lab was, of course, much larger than her teeny little office. And it was buzzing with a few grad students who barely looked up as they walked in, then went back to whatever they were working on.

"Can I get you to set it on the scale?"

Xenia lifted it out of her bag, and handed it to the doctor instead.

"Wow, that's not nearly as heavy as I expected,"

down in her chair. She pressed her hands to her skirts,

he commented as he set it down on the scale himself. "It's mass and appearance suggests something much heavier."

She nodded.

Speaking would be lost on him. He was in the zone. She recognized the look from one her ex-husband used to get when work was more important than she was.

He'd been a doctor, too.

"Hmm. Well, it looks basically just like your average diorite, but it should weigh much, much more. You said you found this under your bed?"

Xenia nodded again. "After it crashed through my roof, my 2nd floor, and my bed."

Dr. Zachary raised a brow.

Forget it, he was absolutely hot.

"And it looked just like this when you found it?"

"Actually, it was kind of pinkish when I found it. I couldn't see it in the dark, so I turned on the light and looked at it in shadows. It didn't exactly glow, but..."

"Huh."

"Yeah."

Xenia and the doctor stared at the rock for another few minutes in silence, and then...

"I have an idea."

She looked at him curiously. "An idea?"

He nodded. "An idea. Mind if I drop this?"

Xenia shrugged. "It's your floor. It did quite a bit of damage to mine. Speaking of which, I need to remember to call the insurance company today."

He used a finger to roll the rock from the scale to

making sure they lay flat against her thighs. She learned

the floor.

The black fell off.

"What the heck is that," Xenia said after jumping away from the gravel that exploded away from her football-shaped black rock.

It wasn't black anymore.

Now it was just...rose colored.

Dr. Zachary picked up the rose-tinted stone with significantly more effort than he'd sent it to the floor.

Xenia watched black pieces of gravel start to fall towards the ceiling.

That is, they were floating.

"It's a xenolith," he said quietly. The entire lab had gone silent, in fact, and all eyes were on them. "A rock fragment embedded within another rock type."

"Yeah, that doesn't help. What *is* it?"

"I have no idea."

The entire room stood and stared at the rose colored rock on the counter in the lab of Dr. Zachary.

And watched it start to move.

the gesture from her aunt, and she admired her Aunt

Mathilda more than any other adult she'd ever known,

Y is for...year

er Year had started.

Yuengling was packed and was standing on the transport deck with fifty or so other young women of about the same age. They all were very similar—beautiful, healthy, and all able to bear children. They varied in height, weight, appearance, and were of wildly different backgrounds, however.

It was better to send out a wide sampling, and the other colonies would do the same.

She wondered about the young woman who would come to take her place in her family, her job, and try to find a mate for herself. She wondered if her mother would smother the Pollinate as she often did Yuengling.

even more than her teacher.

Probably. Her mother smothered everyone. Her friends had all received the treatment before they left for their Years as Pollinates.

Yuengling had left her parents at the gate, as did the rest of the young women. The only people now on deck were the Pollinates along with the six ships that would take them to the other colonies.

The skies would be busy today.

"Please board your designated craft."

Fifty-some hands reached down to grab the one bag of personal items they'd been allowed to bring. Their host families would provide them with everything they would need for their visit, often from their own daughter's closets, as each Pollinate tended to be matched with the family of someone of similar body size. It made the entire thing less stressful on everyone's pocketbook.

Yuengling boarded the craft closest to her, it's hull marked with the evidence of the wars that had concluded forty years before. Now, it was a different world.

She would even go so far as to call it peaceful.

Inside it had been refitted to carry passengers instead of soldiers and other wartime equipment. Yuengling had an assigned seat in a row to herself.

There were only eight of them on a transport designed to seat thirty.

She didn't know any of the other young women.

Taking her seat silently, she set her bag down next to her and immediately started staring out the window.

¶   She didn't notice the red streaks her blood-covered

Soon the transport bay doors would open, and she would get her very first look at the world outside.

She'd never seen anything outside of the colony walls in her entire life.

Admittedly, she was only nineteen, not really old enough to have even had a chance to see outside, but still, she felt like she had been ready for this for ages already.

She had stared out the "window" in her room every day of her life. She watched the screen that showed her what they had decided forty years ago would be the best thing for the residents of Cylinder 14, what the landscape might have looked like before the war. They felt that those who had managed to live through the horrible years of death and pain deserved some brightness and joy instead of the dead depression that was reality of the landscape.

But four decades had passed now, and things would have grown back. There would be a new landscape, and Yuengling was dying to see it.

"Prepare for launch," the same tin voice from before announced as the engines began to ramp up for takeoff.

Yuengling was greatly disappointed to see shields lower over the window she'd just been looking out before the bay doors had a chance to raise.

"No," she whispered as the screen that had lowered over her window flickered to life, showing a bright, cheery version of what she'd just been staring at outside. On the screen the bay doors opened, and she

hands left when she wiped them on her white dress.

saw what she'd stared at her entire life. "Damn it."

She heard similar sounds of disappointment from behind her, and turned her head. She could just see that the young woman behind her was sulking.

"What do they think they have to keep protecting us from," Yuengling wondered out loud in the pouter's direction.

"I've been wondering that myself since the day I was born. It's time to get out of these damn towers, already."

"What do you think you're doing right now," a third young woman who probably wore her anger on her face like she did in her voice spoke up. "You're getting out, you just can't see anything on the way. You know, for all they tell us, we might not even be going anywhere. I mean, can you feel yourself moving? How do we know we've even left the hangar?"

Two others mumbled agreement from behind, and Yuengling craned her head as far as she could to see who had spoken. She couldn't remove her restraining harness—it had locked into place with the lowering of the view screens outside her window.

"Why would they lie to us, though," Yuengling asked out loud. She'd never thought of that possibility. She'd just wanted to see what she was missing, even if it was still charred and dead land. It would allow her, and others, to appreciate even more what the people before her had created, if that was the case.

"So we'll go willingly to the slaughter, that's why," the pouting woman behind her said sharply. "You don't

She didn't look at the broken body of the sewer rat that

actually think we're leaving to get pregnant by some foreign colonist, do you?"

Of course she did, although she didn't say so. Several of the other young women started laughing cynically, obviously in on some bad joke that had passed Yuengling by.

Thankfully she didn't need to reveal her naivety, because someone else did it for her.

"Of course that's what we're here for. You see the other Pollinates coming for their Years all the time, just when our girls leave."

"Those aren't young women. Those are their soldiers and spies, placed among us so when it comes time to reveal the truth they'll be ready to suppress any uprising."

Yuengling's head was spinning, and another voice answered the question in her head before she could ask it out loud.

"Why do you think such a small percentage of our women come back home? They aren't choosing to stay, they've been forced to stay wherever they've been taken. And the few that do choose that life have probably just been the most susceptible to brainwashing. They used to have a name for that—Stockholm Syndrome."

Yuengling wanted to drown out the voices. She had by all accounts lived a very sheltered life. Her parents allowed her privileges that other girls didn't always have. She was kept out of the public school sessions, instead taught by her father at home. Her friends were similarly sheltered, but had all been called for their

she'd been playing with a few minutes before.

Years before she had.

And then she didn't have a chance to think any more. The ship they were on shuddered as it hit something.

Or as something hit it.

"Please remain seated," the tin voice said calmly. "Please place the breathing masks over your face when they descend from the ceiling."

No.

"No," Yuengling whispered. Something her father had taught her when she was very young flashed into the forefront of her mind surrounded by alarms and a violent nauseating reaction. "NO!"

"What the hell," the young woman who had seemed to have all the answers responded. "You want us to die?"

"No, don't put the masks on! They're...they'll kill you. Don't put them on!" Yuengling didn't know how she know, but she heard her father's voice repeating over and over in her head to never put on a mask when instructed. There was more, but her father's voice faded. She couldn't remember...

"Whatever, I'm not going down because you don't know what's really going on," the other young woman replied, slipping the mask on over her face. "Where the hell did you go to school? They always drilled us..."

And she slumped over, mid-sentence.

The ship gave another violent jerk.

Yuengling couldn't see any of other girls except for the girl who was sitting behind her, but she knew they'd heard her.

¶ A small window on her brightly painted door slid

The breathing masks all hung loose from the ceiling, bouncing and swaying from their plastic tubes.

"Are you sure," the woman behind her asked. "Are you sure it's death? How do you know?"

"I don't remember now," Yuengling replied, loudly enough that the other girls could hear her over the klaxon that was now sounding. "But I knew once. My father taught me…"

Her voice ended as a scream as she felt the bottom fall out of her seat, the shoulder straps of her harness pulling her down. Others screamed as well, until…

All of their voices were cut off as the ship hit ground and the breath was knocked out of them all. Yuengling's harness was broken, and she was flung out of her seat and over into the next row. She saw someone else flying through the air as her hair obscured her vision for a moment.

The siren shut off, and it was quiet.

Someone moaned, but another hushed her quickly.

Yuengling tested her limbs, and when she decided nothing had broken, she flipped her feet down to the floor and turned herself right side up.

Cautiously she poked her head up so she could look around the cabin, when she saw it.

All the screens covering the windows had been shattered, but one had broken off completely. Ducking through the rows, Yuengling rushed as quickly as she could to the other side of the cabin.

She saw nothing like the screens had ever shown.

aside, and she could see her teacher's smiling face.

There were trees and tall grasses everywhere, growing wild and thick where they had crashed to the ground.

And then she saw people—at least she thought they were people—dressed in clothing that blended nearly perfectly with the surrounding vegetation, walking towards the ships.

With weapons.

Yuengling heard the hiss before any of the others.

"The gas," she said loudly. "They've turned on the gas. We were supposed to breathe it in and be dead already, but we're not. They're trying to kill us now."

"I'm stuck in my seat still," someone said from the back of the ship. "I can't get out!"

Yuengling looked around frantically, and then remembered something her father had given her for the trip. A toy, he'd said. Something to remember home by. Not good for much except looking at.

Except...

Yuengling ran back to where she'd been seated and found her bag. Rustling around in it, she heard someone coughing.

"Tie off the cords on the masks," she commanded as she pulled the very old tube from her bag. It was a cylinder that was supposed to look like her colony from the outside, Cylinder 14. She twisted it, and the bottom fell to the ground, broken.

A knife.

She ran to the pouting girl who was now looking rather frightened, and quickly cut the belts holding her in place. "Help anyone out who's out of their seats.

¶ "Jane, may I come in?"

Tie off the mask cords for anyone who can't do it themselves."

"Yeah, sure, okay."

Yuengling rushed around the cabin, releasing everyone she could.

Two had died when they put their masks on, one when her neck snapped with the landing.

Four young women and Yuengling made their way to the hatch that had allowed them entrance only a few minutes before.

She hit the emergency release, which thankfully hadn't been disabled or broken in the crash.

The door flew open, and five young women were face to face with fifteen armed men and women.

People not from the colonies.

Fourteen guns trained on Yuengling's face, and four young women behind her cowered for cover.

One young man with a gun stepped forward.

"We've been waiting for you, Yuengling."

That's right, they were. And Yuengling was ready for them. After all, her father had taught her to survive.

It was going to be one hell of a Year.

¶ "Yes, you may come in, teacher," she responded

politely. It was always important to use your manners,

$\mathcal{Z}$ is for...zombie

Zanie got home from work a little later than usual that day. She had been in a bit of an accident. You could never simply walk away from an accident, she had discovered. There were always complications.

Usually the police were involved. There was paperwork. Fines. Blame was assigned.

Not this time.

There were no more police.

Paperwork was pointless when there wasn't anyone left who cared enough to file it.

Blame? Well, how could you blame a bird for singing?

Not that Zanie had been attacked by a bird who refused to stop it's song.

Aunt Mathilda had always told her. Polite children

No, Zanie had been bit.

It had been about time, really. She had been fighting against the undead for so long, it was a miracle she hadn't succumbed before now. Months, or years maybe, of shooting, slashing, smashing...a whole lot of "essing".

Once she was bit, the fight went right out of her. Bluntblade, her partner for the day, quickly dispatched her attacker in a great display of blood. His sword had sliced through the air, completely removing the undead's head in a spectacular manner. And he looked at her, asking if she was all right.

The large wound on her neck should have been answer enough.

But she hadn't given him a chance to get rid of her in a similar manner. She didn't bite him, but she did put a rather large hole in his chest.

It had been instinct. Kill the ones trying to kill you, whether they were racing for your jugular or raising a gun to your temple. That's what had kept her alive these past few...well, since the breakdown. Who knew how long it had been? It didn't matter now anyway.

She walked away from the place she had been calling home with her fellow fighters and instead went towards the apartment she had shared with her fiance.

Before.

The route was not without it's own perils. She saw an absurd amount of people who had been turned before she had. It would have paralyzed her just yesterday. An hour ago.

didn't get hit, or yelled at. It hadn't always worked at

Honestly, she had never seen this many undead in one place ever. There were hundreds. Could she remember fighting more than ten at a time?

And instead of terror, the buzz of adrenaline surging through her and bringing her to attention, she felt lethargic. Sluggish. No one looked at her, and she felt it difficult to look at them, either.

Despite the missing limbs on those who had encountered killers like her and escaped, missing faces from those who had gotten in fights with other undead, and the ragged, desperate appearance of just about everyone, Zanie kept walking. And eventually, she reached her old apartment.

Home. It was ravaged on the outside. The signs of looters and vandals let loose on society when things had looked their worst had taken their toll on their cute building in the family-oriented neighborhood. The doors were no longer locked.

Surprisingly, things inside were much better. Signs of wear were evident, there was blood on the walls and floors where the old, young and infirm had not been quick enough for escape, but her apartment was relatively untouched.

It didn't matter that any food had already been looted.

Zanie wasn't going to need to eat it any more.

It didn't matter that her closet had been rummaged through, and her good hiking boots had apparently been filched.

Zanie didn't expect to need them for long, anyway.

home, of course, but Jane pushed that thought away

In her bedroom, stepping over what was left of the man she had once promised to marry, Zanie looked at her reflection in the mirror. She was not surprised to see a glassy-eyed woman stare back at her, eyes smudged and looking as if she hadn't slept for weeks. That was pretty much her standard appearance lately.

What surprised her was that the wound on her neck was...not nearly as bad as it had felt when she'd been bitten. And her eyes, while glassy, we're still her eyes. They hadn't taken on that animal look, the reflecting look that gave the undead away.

Slowly, over her ex-fiance again, and to the bathroom, she tried the water. Of course it wasn't working. But the toilet still had water, and taking a dusty hand towel she dipped it into the tank, avoiding as much green muck as she could, and started wiping at the blood on her neck.

It all came off. Almost all. There was still a spot that looked like a bullet wound, but she looked very closely.

It was closing.

The sound of her own scream was more alarming than anything else she'd seen so far. Scarier than the sight of hundreds of undead all in one area, worse than walking right through the midst of creatures who usually wanted to rip her throat out, was the sound of her actual scream. Not the distorted roar that came from the throats of every single recently turned human she had ever seen.

Zanie jerked back, and stumbled out of the

and concentrated on her smile. It worked here, and so

bathroom, clutching the towel. She stumbled back through her apartment, just as she had done after killing Simon when he had come after her. Except now she was running from herself.

Outside, they were everywhere. There were thousands. Where had they come from? Why were they here?

Why were they all staring at her?

She stood in the doorway. They were silent. The entire world was silent.

A flash of movement caught the corner of her eye. Someone, an undead, was walking around the corner towards her, but her gaze went to her reflection in the window of the abandoned car.

Now her eyes shone.

"Welcome home," the undead said in a voice that was more a growl than anything else. Her gaze snapped to his eyes that shone just like hers. Like every member of the hoard before her. "My queen."

Zanie watched as the thousands before her all fell on their knees.

And then she wondered if maybe it wasn't worth living with these undead things after all.

she would remember *all* of Aunt Mathilda's lessons.

Nickified

*N*icki Ivey is an author and publisher of short stories and novels. She has volunteered as the Municipal Liaison for the Lehigh Valley region of National Novel Writing Month since 2008, and has been writing as a participant of the event since 2003. This collection of short stories is her first print publication through Ivey Books.